"Ariel, I've m...

"Too late."

"Why?" Pete murmured.

"It's just too late," she insisted, squirming within the circle of his arm and facing the car to push the key into the lock.

"It's never too late," he whispered against her neck.

She let her body go soft against his. Facing him, responding, was the easy way. She fought for the strength to choose the more difficult path. "Don't count on what isn't going to happen."

"Because you don't care?" Pete slid his hand up from her waist, pressed his mouth against her hair. He inhaled her scent for a second, but no longer. He knew he was hurting her.

Her pulse pounded at her temples, and she moaned softly and laid her forehead against the car window. She was losing....

Dear Reader,

Each and every month, to meet your sophisticated standards, to satisfy your taste for substantial, memorable, emotion-packed novels of life and love, of dreams and possibilities, Silhouette brings you six extremely **Special Editions**.

Soon these exclusive editions will sport a new, updated cover look—our way of marking Silhouette **Special Editions'** continually renewed commitment to bring you the very best and the brightest in romance writing.

Keep an eye out for the new Silhouette **Special Edition** covers—inside you'll find a soul-satisfying selection of love stories penned by your favorite Silhouette authors and by some dazzling new writers destined to become tomorrow's romance stars.

And don't forget the two Silhouette *Classics* at your bookseller's each month—the most beloved Silhouette **Special Editions** and Silhouette *Intimate Moments* of yesteryear, now reissued by popular demand.

Today's bestsellers, tomorrow's *Classics*—that's Silhouette **Special Editions**. And soon, we'll be looking more special than ever!

From all the authors and editors of Silhouette **Special Editions**,

Warmest Wishes,

Leslie Kazanjian
Senior Editor

JENNIFER MIKELS
Remember the Daffodils

Silhouette Special Edition

Published by Silhouette Books New York

America's Publisher of Contemporary Romance

To a special lady,
my editor, Alice Alfonsi.

SILHOUETTE BOOKS
300 East 42nd St., New York, N.Y. 10017

ISBN: 0-373-09478-7

First Silhouette Books printing September 1988

Printed in the U.S.A.

Books by Jennifer Mikels

Silhouette Special Edition

A Sporting Affair #66
Whirlwind #124
Remember the Daffodils #478

Silhouette Romance

Lady of the West #462
Maverick #487
Perfect Partners #511
The Bewitching Hour #551

JENNIFER MIKELS

uses her extensive travel experience as research for her writing. She's ventured all over the East Coast, Canada and practically every northern state and loved every minute of it. Her home base is Phoenix, Arizona, where she, her husband and their two sons share a love of the West, the country and mountain camping.

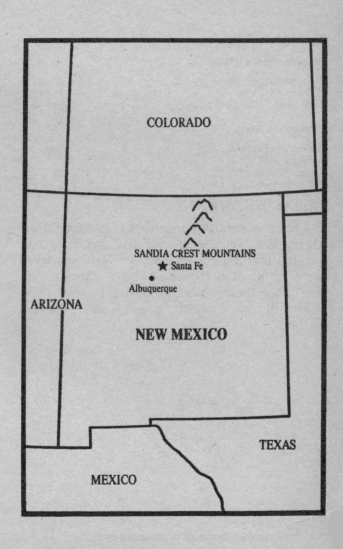

Prologue

Yellow daffodils." Ariel Hammond stared at the flowers nestled in the florist's box amid leaves and leaves of green tissue.

"I've never known any man who sent yellow daffodils to a woman." Rosie Caron turned toward Ariel, a puzzled expression lining her face. "Roses, if she's lucky. Carnations, sometimes. But daffodils?"

Ariel dragged her gaze from the bouquet toward Rosie's round face.

Rosie was a short, dark-haired woman in her early thirties. During the ten months that she'd worked as a part-time shop assistant for Ariel at the Potpourri Bazaar, she'd exhibited an outgoing nature and the gift of gab. She was nosy, endearing, and overly romantic.

"He must be special." The speculation in Rosie's voice matched the anticipation in her dark eyes.

Ariel avoided her stare and turned away, responding to the swish of the door opening.

The warmth of a summer day swept into the shop as a customer sauntered in. The heavy rose fragrance of the woman's perfume rivaled the scent of incense from a nearby counter display of candles.

Ariel gestured toward the woman. "Rosie, would you...?"

"Sure. But Ariel, those are your favorite flowers, aren't they? Who sent them?" she whispered.

"Later."

As Rosie whirled around to serve the woman, Ariel reached into the florist's box for the card. She didn't need to read it; she knew who'd sent the flowers. Only one man knew her favorite flower: Pete Turner.

Stalling before she had to acknowledge his presence in her life again, she cradled the box in her arm and ambled toward the storeroom at the back of the shop. There she set the box on a table and stepped around crates of recently delivered imports to open the back door.

Clouds drifted over the sun, offering relief to the tourists who strolled the cobblestone streets of Albuquerque near Old Town. When those visitors completed their tour of the galleries and craft shops housed in the nineteenth-century adobe buildings, they'd wander back toward the parking lot. Often the unique imports in the display window of the Potpourri Bazaar caught their eye and encouraged a stroll down the street toward her store.

Ariel drew a deep breath, telling herself that she should be thinking about business. Instead her mind kept recalling the image of a tall, dark-haired man. She looked back over her shoulder at the box of daffodils.

After four years, why had he had to leave New York? Why had he sent her flowers?

Tension fluttered in her stomach as she slipped the card out of the envelope and read the message.

There's a Chinese proverb that states: Once you meet someone you like, you're destined to meet again.

Pete

Damn him. Ariel frowned at the card in her hand. If he thought he could waltz back into her life after all these years, he was in for a rude awakening.

"Well?" Rosie asked so suddenly that Ariel jumped at the sound of her voice. "Who are the flowers from?" Rosie took an impatient stance. "Come on, Ariel, I told you before anyone else that I planned to go back to school in the fall. I made you my confidante and—"

"You want me to return the honor," Ariel said lightly.

"Please."

"You're nosy."

"Yes, I know."

"And not regretful."

"Hardly ever."

Ariel laughed and released a resigned sigh. "An old friend sent the flowers."

"Boyfriend?"

"Friend."

"That sounds dull."

Far from it, Ariel reflected, unwilling to reveal to Rosie the closeness that she and Pete had shared. Too easily, she could recall the sensuous softness of Pete's voice when he'd whispered in her ear for too many nights during too many months.

"Where has he been?"

"New York." Ariel swung away from the door. "He moved there several years ago. He's back in Albuquerque."

Rosie cocked a brow.

"The firm he works for sent him here to open a new office."

"Ah, so he's back because of business?"

"Yes," Ariel said firmly, needing to remind herself of that. "And I haven't even seen him yet."

"Then how do you know?"

"My mother told me."

Rosie gave her head a quick shake. "He saw your mother first?"

Ariel smiled. "No. My mother is dating his father."

"Sounds like a soap opera."

"Doesn't it? Even the heroine's life is full of trouble," she added, looking past Rosie and staring at the front door of the shop.

During the night someone had hurled a rock. It had crashed into the beveled and etched stained glass above the door, cracking the intricate floral design.

This morning she'd dealt with the handiwork of a vandal. During lunch her mother had announced that she was dating Evan Turner. And now... Her gaze returned to the daffodils. And now she knew that Pete was back.

Didn't she have enough trouble? Wasn't it enough for a woman to act the fool over a man once in her life? Did she have to be tested a second time? Surely the hurt and wanting didn't exist anymore, she mused.

Ariel slammed the shop door. Sure, it did.

Chapter One

You're dating Virginia Hammond?" Concern edged Pete's voice. "She's not exactly your type, is she, Dad?" He ran a knife along the tape of a mover's carton and then looked up when his father failed to respond. "Dad, are you listening to me?"

"Yes." Evan swiveled the wing-back chair away from his son's desk and stared out the large window, which had a view of the sprawling city. "Why isn't she?"

"She's flaky."

Evan scowled. "Like her daughter?"

Pete flipped up the carton flaps. "At times Ariel was kooky."

"May I remind you that at one time that kooky lady made your heart go pitter-patter?"

Pete ignored his father's comment. "We aren't discussing my relationship with Ariel. We're discussing your—"

"*You're* discussing it, not me." Evan pushed himself out of the chair. "I suppose I should help you. Why is it that you've been here almost a week and you still haven't finished unpacking?" Evan scanned the family room, which had a cathedral ceiling. "Is this just a temporary position in Albuquerque?"

"No, I plan on staying. When I took the position with Bryant and Bryant, I visualized settling back here one day."

Evan grinned. "And you persuaded J.C. Bryant that he needed an office in New Mexico?"

"It wasn't easy, or I'd have been back here sooner." Pete glanced at his father, who continued to frown at the disorder in the room. "And I didn't have time to unpack. The office demanded my attention first." Pete bent forward to lift a lamp from the mover's carton. "About Virginia Hammond."

"The mother is as charming as I recall her daughter was."

"Where did you meet her?"

"At your apartment. She was making something with tofu, and you were reading directions about how to use a wok."

"Not the daughter." Pete sighed exasperatedly. When Pete had flown in from New York at Christmastime, his father hadn't been dating Virginia Hammond. If their romance wasn't more than a few months old, it couldn't be serious, Pete reasoned. Yet Evan seemed to be afflicted already with Virginia's scatterbrained manner. "The mother. Where did you meet her?"

"A lovely woman," Evan responded softly, sounding smitten.

Slowly, Pete looked over his shoulder. He might already be too late, he realized, wondering if logic would even work with his father at this point.

Evan beamed, then shrugged when Pete didn't respond. "You haven't been back in Albuquerque one week, Peter. Don't you have more important things to think about than your old dad's love life?" Evan insisted, eyeing a sculpture and rotating it in his hand. "How did you convince J.C. Bryant that he needed a financial consultant's office here?"

Pete peered over the top of a lampshade and screwed it on. "Bryant and Bryant has several offices all over the country. Why wouldn't they want one in New Mexico?"

Evan laughed. "That sounds to me as if you gave them a fantastic sell job."

"I did my best. But everything isn't as wonderful as it sounds. The PR people in New York were contacted by a business magazine. One of their reporters will be here in a few days. She's doing articles on several Southwest and West Coast consulting firms."

-"Including yours?"

"Right."

A frown creased Evan's forehead. "I'd think you'd be pleased. Publicity of that sort is bound to attract new clients."

"Publicity of what sort? The staff of that magazine digs. Though a write-up in their magazine does offer a seal of approval—" he paused and grimaced "—they don't hesitate to disclose everything."

"What could they possibly find out about you? And for half a century Bryant and Bryant has had an impeccable reputation, hasn't it?"

Pete set the lamp on an end table. "I'm not worried about that, but I wish this reporter were arriving later, after I have everything organized. If something goes wrong, it's more likely to happen now, while I'm struggling to get the firm established here."

"You worry too much."

"I've worked too hard to blow this chance now."

Evan glanced around for a suitable place to display a Rodin. "What chance?"

"A senior consultant's position."

Evan's head snapped up. "You expect it?"

"I'm hoping for it."

Evan grinned pridefully at his son. "That would be quite an accomplishment at your age."

Pete nodded absently, distracted by a brown carton amid a roomful of the mover's white ones. "What's this?"

"Some things you left at home. I didn't think you'd want them shipped to New York. But now that you're back—well, you might as well collect your treasures."

Pete slanted a look at him. "Or junk," he returned, flipping open the carton flaps. He grinned at the sight of a high school yearbook.

"Nostalgia time?" Evan asked.

"Looks that way." Pete squatted beside the carton and lifted high school mementos from it. He set the yearbook on a chair, then studied a photograph of his college baseball team. Digging back into the carton, his fingers closed over a framed photograph.

Evan ambled closer to stand behind his son. Peering over Pete's shoulder, Evan smiled at the photograph in Pete's hand. "She and her mother have similar looks. Same coppery red hair, soft sparkling-eyed look, delicate features."

Pete frowned, regretting too many things about Ariel. He'd called her kooky. She wasn't. She was a person who had a distinct style of her own. "Do you know how she is?"

"Fine, I assume. I haven't seen a great deal of her. She's been in Ginnie's flower shop a few times. Ariel's store is next door."

"I know."

"You do?" Evan bent forward slightly to see his son's face better. "If your office is near the college, then how...?"

"I drove around the city yesterday."

"And you didn't see her?"

"No." A frown knitted Pete's brow. When had their conversation shifted from his father's love life to his own?

Evan stepped away and touched a painting hanging on the wall. It was a mountain scene, a serene landscape and a favorite of Pete's, which he'd hung in his New York apartment because the scene had reminded him of home, of camping...of Ariel.

"You never said," Evan began, stepping back from the painting and squinting at it, "whether you were surprised when I wrote you about her divorce." He nudged a corner of the frame to straighten it.

"I was more surprised that she got married. Marriage is the last thing I thought she wanted." Pete stared at the photograph. A candid shot, it revealed her lighthearted spirit as she stood in white shorts and a striped top holding on to the rigging of a Windsurfer. "She talked about traveling," he responded, staring at her wind-tossed hair, remembering her laughter as she'd brushed the hair from her eyes long enough for him to take the photograph.

"So why did she marry within six months after you left for New York?"

That question had nagged Pete for months. Ariel had always talked of playing the vagabond and touring Europe. Why had she settled down in California to a Yuppie life-style with a banker, a man she'd barely known?

"Pete?"

Pete shrugged and set her photograph back in the box along with the others and the yearbook. "I don't know." As he closed the flaps of the carton he again considered the direction of the conversation. Somehow Evan had steered Pete off the subject of one Hammond woman and onto another. "Where did you meet Virginia Hammond, Dad?"

"You are amazingly single-minded. Were you always like that?" Evan questioned in an amazed tone.

"Always," Pete assured him, rising to his feet. "Well? Where?"

"At the college."

"She's taking one of your classes?" Pete asked, puzzled. "Why would she want to learn about medieval history?"

"Son, there is always a need for new knowledge." Evan's voice deepened. The pedantic tone usually preceded a lecture about something.

Pete dodged it with a quick question. "So she was one of your students last semester?"

"I never said that, Pete."

"Dad, will you please make sense?"

"I will if you'll stop asking the questions and then answering them yourself."

Pete gave his head a quick shake. "Okay. Let's start over. You met her at the college?"

"Yes."

"In one of your classes, *professor*?"

"No."

Pete heard the chuckle in his father's voice. "Then where at the college did you meet her?"

"At the college theater."

"At a play?"

"Yes."

"So you were watching a play and conveniently sitting beside her and she—"

"You're doing it again."

"What am I doing again?"

"Answering before you ask the question. It's good you never took a class from me. I'd have insisted on your withdrawal. No professor likes a know-it-all in his class, Peter."

Pete touched his forehead and rubbed at the pounding pain between his brows. Why was this conversation taking half a dozen different directions? When had his father adopted Virginia's helter-skelter manner of thinking? "Would you please tell me why you were at the theater?"

"As a consultant."

"What do you know about acting?"

"Nothing, of course."

"I'll bite, Dad," Pete returned as he strolled into the kitchen. "What were you consulting about?"

"History," Evan yelled out.

Pete yanked open a drawer and grabbed the aspirin bottle. Quickly he tossed two pills into his mouth, using the muddy brew at the bottom of his coffee cup as a chaser. A bitter taste clung to his tongue, and his headache seemed worse than before, but his father was beginning to make sense.

Why had it taken him so long to reach this point? Pete wondered. Evan Turner was the man who'd raised him, shown him how to fly a kite, patiently spent hours demonstrating the correct way to knot a tie, and lectured him on the downfalls of steaming up car windows at the drive-in. He was the man whose thinking paralleled Pete's about foreign policy, transplant operations, and financial investments.

Now nearly five minutes had passed before Pete had been able to make sense of his father's words. Pete paused in the doorway and braced a hand against the doorjamb. "The college is doing a medieval play?"

"Not exactly."

Pete sighed heavily. *Back to square one.*

"During the summer months, several amateur thespians perform plays there. Virginia is a volunteer with the woman's hospital auxiliary. For a fund-raiser, they're putting on a play. She's like a candy striper at the hospital."

A pink-and-white striped uniform suited the woman who acted as if she'd stepped out of a fairy tale, Pete thought as he plopped down on the nearest chair and rested his forearms on his thighs. "Are you being deliberately dense?"

"As a matter of fact, I am."

A sense of relief washed over Pete. For a moment he had thought his father had developed a new way of thinking. The unemployment line would certainly have followed. Dense professors rarely kept their faculty positions. "Why?"

"Because I came over to help you unpack and to share some wonderful news with you, and immediately you launched into a diatribe about this woman's character."

"All I said was that she's as kooky as Ariel is." *Flakier*, Pete thought, but knew better than to offer that observation.

His father's feelings for Ariel's mother were more intense than Pete had first realized. And now Pete sensed he'd hurt his father. "I'm sorry."

"Apology accepted."

"I think it's great that you've found someone you can have a good time with. But she's so different from the type of woman—"

Evan cut him off. "My feelings for Ginnie aren't quite so casual. I want more than a—" he paused and then finished in a disdainful tone "—*good time* with her. That's why I came to talk to you. I didn't want to spring anything on you."

"Spring? Spring what? Are you telling me you're serious about her? You might marry her?" Pete fell back in his chair.

Having Virginia Hammond for a stepmother would mean holidays with her encouraging everyone to make Easter hats out of newspapers and participate in egg hunts. It would mean green soup on St. Patrick's Day and barbecues in the snow.

Pete shook his head, feeling the same disbelief that he'd felt when he'd sat in Ariel's living room and she'd shared such family memories with him.

"Peter," Evan said impatiently, assuring his son that he was repeating himself, "it's very possible."

"Dad, you hardly know her."

"I know her very well. I told you that we met at the theater."

"Right. You were consulting." Pete struggled to sound calm. "And what was she doing?"

"Acting."

Playing Tinker Bell? Pete wondered. She'd suit such a role. He recalled the petite woman with brilliant red hair waltzing around her kitchen and in and out of rooms as if her feet never touched the ground.

Pete didn't dislike her. In fact, he thought, recalling the times when he'd been at the Hammond home and visited Ariel, he'd laughed often at her mother's breezy attitude. Her disjointed conversations had held him captive with amusement as she'd breathlessly jumped nonstop from one topic to another.

But that woman wasn't right for Professor Evan Turner, the sedate, distinguished-looking, silver-haired member of the history staff. She'd have the faculty at the small conservative New Mexico college gaping if she arrived at a faculty dinner wearing one of her outlandish getups.

"Pete?"

He refocused on his father's face. "Which play are they doing?"

"*The Taming of the Shrew.* Ginnie is quite impressive as the gentle Bianca."

Despite his logical objections to such a mismatch as Virginia and his father, a smile tugged the edges of Pete's lips. An unfamiliar warmth could be heard in his father's voice. The man was in love.

Falling in love with a Hammond wasn't difficult. When Pete had first noticed Ariel, she'd been acting in the same play, sashaying across the stage, rifling insults at Petruchio in front of a college audience.

Pete had watched, spellbound.

Hammond women dazzled. They also flitted through life, Pete reminded himself. They were impulsive and unconcerned with consequences.

"Has Virginia told Ariel?" Pete asked, crossing the room to the massive oak desk by the window. He pulled a folder from his briefcase. He needed to brief himself before tomorrow on a client's financial situation.

"Ariel already knows that we're seeing each other."

Pete nodded and looked down, grabbing a pencil and nervously twirling it between his fingers as he wondered if anything he could say would prevent Evan from rushing into something he'd regret.

Pete recalled how he'd struggled for weeks before he'd finally forced himself to break off with Ariel. Even then he'd ached for months just to hear her voice. He'd sat in his New York apartment, imagining his life as it would be if she'd been with him. Logic had warred with his feelings for her. He'd kept himself from calling her, knowing that she'd have been miserable with the life he could have offered in New York.

"Virginia hasn't said this to me, but I think she's concerned that Ariel might have bad feelings toward all of the Turner men."

The pencil in Pete's hand stilled. He stared at the geometric shapes he'd doodled in the margin of a corporate statement. Quickly he rubbed the eraser across the paper. A moment of thinking about Ariel and he was screwing up his best client's asset sheet. What was it about her and her mother that aroused the dreamer in a man?

Pete tossed down the pencil.

"I know what you're thinking," Evan said, "No fool like an old fool."

Young men fall, too, Pete mused. For the right woman. "You're not old."

"Clever, Peter."

"What's that?"

"Avoiding the word fool." Evan slipped his glasses forward and rubbed the bridge of his nose.

"I don't think you're one."

"Quite honestly, neither do I. Ginnie—she makes me laugh. She's so optimistic."

"Rose-colored glasses offer that view." The faint tension in his father's face kept Pete from airing more of his opinion. Through those colorful lenses a tall, good-looking intelligent man who was holding a respected professor's position appeared a perfect catch. But Evan's life-style insisted on a certain propriety that clashed with Virginia's offbeat ideas.

Shouldering the responsibility of raising a son by himself should have taught his father that. Didn't he remember when his wife had fled their marriage, leaving him with a seven-year-old son? Didn't he remember the sorrow of knowing that she'd run off to pursue a love affair with a man almost ten years younger than she? On a whim, she'd abandoned them. Despite one love affair after another, she'd never found the happiness she'd sought. The few times Pete had seen her before her death, she'd spoken of forgiveness. As a man, Pete had been able to accept her remorse, but the childhood pain had never disappeared completely. She'd hurt him and his father badly. Pete didn't want to see his father suffer that same heartache again.

"Ginnie makes me smile more."

Pete understood that. He'd laughed more with Ariel than any other woman he'd ever known. But he'd had the good sense to walk away from her, knowing they'd be at odds. While he'd wanted to scale corporate walls, she'd yearned to stroll past meadows of edelweiss and paddle down the Nile. He'd loved her too much not to let her go.

Evan sat on a crate marked Fragile. "You could use a woman in your life. Then you wouldn't be so preoccupied with mine."

The bluntness of the comment made Pete smile. "How do you know there isn't one?"

Evan frowned suddenly. "Did you leave someone behind?"

The look in his father's eyes said more than his words conveyed. Pete heard the silent "again."

Most of his life Pete had done everything he could to make his father proud. He'd thought his father had endured the major catastrophe in his life years ago when his wife had left him. Evan didn't need any more pain. Out of love and respect, Pete had worked hard not to cause his father more hurt. He'd been a model son. But he knew his father hadn't understood—maybe never would understand—why Pete had abruptly, coldly, left Ariel and moved to New York.

He'd chosen the only path possible. Ariel had longed for a life filled with new experiences. Pete couldn't drift with her; he'd had his own goals. And just as he would never have fitted into her plans, she'd have detested his life-style, would have hated the quasi-business parties that a consultant's wife was expected to throw as well as attend.

But more than once during those early months in New York he'd considered returning to Albuquerque and telling her that he'd made a mistake. Then before he could, she'd married.

He drew a hard breath. Somehow he'd convinced himself that she'd been wrong for him. But through the years he'd never found any woman better suited to him.

The touch of Evan's hand on his arm caused him to raise his eyes to his father's face.

"Will you see Ariel again?"

Pete shook his head. "I don't know." Despite his answer, he knew he would see her. The chemistry between them insisted on a meeting. She was too near, too tempting, for him not to see her again. He'd known that when he'd ordered the flowers. She wasn't the type of woman who'd fit into his life; she wouldn't want to. She'd never play the gracious hostess, the docile wife whose sole purpose was to support her husband in his career. He'd met wives of other consultants with Bryant and Bryant. They were conservative in their dress, quiet in their manner and speech—and dull. But then every woman he'd met was dull in comparison to Ariel. And not one of them made him think of yellow daffodils.

"Match weed, they're called," Virginia informed her daughter while positioning several clusters of yellow flowers in the bouquet of orange mums. "They're an excellent substitute for baby's breath. Don't you think so?"

As her mother glanced back at her, Ariel eyed the unusual flower arrangement and merely nodded. "Unusual."

"You don't like it." Virginia scurried several steps away from the counter, studied the arrangement, then scanned her flower shop.

Ariel leaned back as her mother whisked by and reached inside a case for a brilliant blue iris.

"I'll pick up some extra hamburger for dinner if you'd like to join Evan and—"

"No," Ariel cut in.

"You need to get out more. It's not healthy to have such a limited social life at twenty-nine. Eighty percent of divorced women find another man within the first three years that they're single again. But they wouldn't if they never went anywhere. That's a known statistic."

Ariel knew all about her mother's known statistics. She made them up.

"Why, thirteen percent of American women suffer from terminal frigidity because they allow one bad experience to influence them. There," she said brightly, stuffing the iris into the bouquet. "Now it has more pizzazz. Adolph's Medley."

"What?"

"That's what I'm making this evening for dinner. Adolph's Medley. I found the recipe on a pamphlet advertising meat tenderizer. It's a wonderful dish of..." She paused thoughtfully. "Well, hamburger is in it. I told Evan I'd surprise him with something different."

Ariel tugged on one kinky curl of her recent permanent. Too tight. The permanent was too tight. Though her hair still brushed her shoulders, the permanent had corkscrewed every strand of her red hair. She caught her reflection in the glass enclosure that housed fresh roses. The hairstyle wasn't unattractive, but for the next three months she could discard every comb she owned.

"I like your hair," Virginia stated, whirling around and smiling at her. "It's different."

Ariel curled one side of her mouth into a sneer. "Isn't it?"

Virginia touched her shoulder in passing. "It will grow out. When it does, it will look lovely." She paused in midstride and looked back at Ariel. "By December, do you think?"

Trained as she was at following her mother's conversation, Ariel stood dumbfounded for a second, then realized they were still discussing her hair. "Are you asking if my permanent will have straightened a little by December?" At Virginia's nod, Ariel assured her, "I'm sure it will have, Mother. Why?"

"Well," she said breezily, offering her back to Ariel again and moving a vase of gladiolus from one shelf to another, "it's pretty this way, but I thought you'd want to wear it up at the wedding."

"What wedding?"

Virginia faced her with a broad smile. "Why, mine, dear."

"Mother, has Evan asked you to marry him?"

"No, not yet. But he will."

Ariel breathed deeply. "Mother, about Evan. He's not..." She hesitated, wondering how to impress her mother with the difficulties of marrying a man so different from her.

Virginia swept a feather duster over a set of duck-shaped vases containing silk roses. "I noticed the new merchandise at your shop." At Ariel's quizzical look, Virginia explained, "The elephant's-head end table in the window?"

"It's a special order. Some woman from Texas with an overabundance of money and little knowledge of art came in and thumbed through my merchandise catalog. She spotted that end table and requested that I order it for her."

"Where is it from?"

"Sidi bou Zid."

Virginia's eyes widened.

"Tunisia."

"It's certainly terrible," Virginia whispered as if concerned about offending someone.

"Yes, it is," Ariel agreed. "When the woman pointed a long, manicured nail at the photograph of that elephant's-head table, I struggled not to laugh. But that's what she wanted."

"You have some interesting customers."

Ariel studied her mother for a long moment. She seemed empty-headed at times. In fact she was terrible at business matters, but she was a master at evasion. Talking about the Potpourri Bazaar had sidetracked Ariel from what she'd really wanted to discuss. "Mother, I'd be really happy for you if you married again."

"Thank you, dear."

"And Evan is a..."

"Delight."

"Yes, I like him," Ariel assured her.

"I'd hoped you did."

Ariel considered her next words. She'd spoken the truth. Evan Turner would make some woman a wonderful husband. And after nine years as a widow, her mother deserved such happiness. Her mother needed a man in her life. Some women did.

Some women longed for a life of baking bread, growing prize-winning roses, and cooking fabulous dinners that impressed a man's colleagues. Ariel had tried that life with a banker whose success had done little to make up for his lack of creativity and imagination.

Even before the divorce had been finalized, she'd sold everything she'd received in the community property settlement, had left California to return to Albuquerque, and had sunk all her money into the Potpourri Bazaar.

After three years of trying to be someone she wasn't, she had the freedom to be herself again. She'd learned a valuable lesson and would never try to be the kind of woman someone else wanted.

And her mother wouldn't succeed at such self-deception, either, whether she knew it or not. Ariel's father had never questioned his wife's idiosyncrasies. He'd accepted her flair for the dramatic, her costumed dinners, and her inability to balance a checkbook. He'd been her perfect match, owning a flower shop and preferring the fragrances of flowers to scaling some corporate ladder and having pockets of money. Throughout Ariel's childhood, he'd shared his dreams of crossing the Sinai, of seeing the Louvre, of sailing the Caribbean. Her mother had shared his dreams. Ariel had, too. They were just dreams, but in her own way, with her store of imports, Ariel felt she'd kept some of them alive.

Ariel believed her mother had taken over the flower shop for the same reason. But Virginia had no disposition for business, and she was no more faculty wife material than Ariel was. Virginia Hammond would be bored in less than a year living with a man who wore traditional professor's tweeds and smoked a pipe.

Ariel watched her mother's hands deftly arranging carnations in a corsage. Deciding on a different angle, Ariel began, "When I married Jonathan, you warned me that he was..."

"Stuffy, dear. Very stuffy."

Ariel laughed. "Yes, he was. And you were right about him. He wasn't flexible. He wanted me to be something I couldn't be. And—"

"You shouldn't have to change for anyone," Virginia said, interrupting. "If he loved you, he'd have accepted you as you are." She pressed small hands to Ariel's cheeks. "Lovable," she added, then rushed to answer the phone.

Ariel wondered if convincing her mother that she was stepping into the same trap was possible. Certainly if she could see how wrong Jonathan had been for her daughter, why couldn't she realize she'd make the same mistake if she married Evan? *Love is blind*, Ariel reflected.

Virginia set down the telephone, scribbling an order for flowers on the pad. "What happened to your store window, Ariel?"

"That happened a few days ago."

"Yes, dear, I noticed it then. But how did it happen?"

"Vandals, I guess," Ariel answered absently.

"It's such a shame. That was a beautiful window, and you'd had it made because you'd liked it so much."

Ariel nodded. She recalled how sick she'd felt when she'd arrived at the shop and had seen the damage.

"Did you call the insurance company?"

"No, I didn't. I decided to take the loss."

Virginia's head snapped up. "For heaven's sake, why?"

"Because I made a claim several weeks ago."

Virginia frowned, then a flicker of acknowledgment sparked in her eyes. "Yes, I remember now. Someone broke into the back of your store and stole a crate, didn't they?"

"Yes."

"You have had such unfortunate luck lately."

Ariel smiled at the sympathy in her mother's voice.

"I'm glad you decided to lease a store so close to mine." A reflective look settled on Virginia's face. "Sometimes, though, I do wish you'd chosen to join me here instead of opening your own store."

Concerned, Ariel frowned. "Why? Do you have problems?"

"Oh, no." Virginia smiled brightly. "But wouldn't it have been lovely to be partners?"

Ariel closed the distance between them. "Mother, I thought you understood. After my marriage, I needed to stand alone. I didn't want to have to answer to anyone."

"That's because he was overbearing."

"Yes, he was. I needed to be independent. I needed to find myself again, and Pop always talked of expanding the flower shop to include exquisite imports."

Virginia's expression softened. "He would have been pleased, Ariel."

Ariel cocked her head quizzically. "But you're not?"

"Of course I am." Virginia disappeared for a second as she reached under the counter for an artificial silver leaf. "Being partners with you was a mother's wishful thinking," she responded. "Since you'd worked here when you were younger and..." Her head popped up. "Mothers always like to keep children close," she added.

"We are close."

"Yes, we are, dear, but I worry about you, too. You've been having so much trouble lately."

"Just kids," Ariel said lightly in an effort to downplay the problem.

"Did the police find out anything about the stolen..." She paused, her expression quizzical. "What was it that they took?"

"Gourds from Peru."

"Odd," Virginia mused. "Why would anyone steal a crate of gourds?"

Ariel shrugged. "I don't know. And no, the police didn't learn anything."

Her mother appeared confused. She'd be even more perplexed if Ariel told her that the crate of broken gourds had been returned with a note, Ariel thought. Aloud, she said, "Mother, you haven't had any problems, have you?" She worried that the trouble might spread to her mother's shop before Ariel decided how to handle the problem.

"No," Virginia assured her, gazing toward the glass case containing fresh roses and orchids. "If vandals got in here, they'd . . ." She shook her head as if refusing the dismal thought. "Well, I'm not even going to think about that."

Unfortunately, Ariel believed that was her mother's biggest fault. She dodged any unpleasantness, refusing to contemplate a problem and solve it before it became insurmountable.

Ariel decided she had to take a firmer stand about Evan. "After what happened with my marriage," she said, leaning on the counter where her mother was working, "why would you want to make a mistake like I did?"

Virginia patted her hand. "Oh, I'd never do that."

"You will be if you marry Evan."

"No, dear."

"Mother, he and his son are two of a kind."

"Yes, you know, I always did like Peter. He had such a wonderful laugh."

"He laughed rarely, Mother."

"Sour grapes. That's not true, and you know it. Why, he always laughed when he was at our house."

Ariel jammed a hand into the pocket of her brightly colored paisley skirt. "But he had a serious side. He was stuffy."

"Peter? Nonsense."

Ariel exhaled deeply. She was getting nowhere.

"If he had been so stuffy, Ariel, you wouldn't have been so heartbroken when he left."

No one could ever deny that Virginia Hammond didn't know how to hit the soft spots. "I thought I loved him. And he didn't love me. I'm grateful, Mother, that he broke off with me."

"But if you'd waited and hadn't married Jonathan so quickly, Peter might have returned sooner. The two of you might have—"

"We weren't right for each other."

"But you felt so bad."

"I recovered. I married Jonathan and—"

"And you cried so much after Peter left," Virginia added, as if the conversation had never shifted away from Pete.

"Yes," Ariel responded quickly. "And cried so much. But if I had been older, I would have realized how much Jonathan wanted what Pete had wanted."

"And what was that?"

"A model wife."

Virginia laughed. "Yes, dear, you're certainly right. You'd never be that."

"But you do see," Ariel stressed, talking slower, "that I didn't realize that."

"And if you had been older," Virginia said more seriously, "you'd have realized all that?"

"Absolutely."

"There you are," Virginia said lightly. "I'm older. I certainly will not make the same mistakes you did, dear. Thank you for that reassurance."

Ariel narrowed an eye at her. She'd been bamboozled by one of the best.

Virginia glanced at the teapot clock on a nearby wall. "Shouldn't you open your store?"

Ariel nodded, deciding to ponder the situation again and think of another approach. Somehow she had to make her mother see what a mistake it would be for her to marry Evan Turner.

"See you later, dear," Virginia called out.

Ariel waved back at her. What agony family gatherings would be if her mother and Evan Turner got married. Pete would be at all of them. Ariel shuddered as she stepped out of her mother's flower shop. That definitely would be the pits.

She took three strides, then stopped cold, frozen at the sight of the short, barrel-chested man standing outside the door of her store.

His lips formed a slow-spreading smile that never reached his eyes. "Ms. Hammond, have you and your mother considered my offer?"

"My mother knows nothing about your *offer*," Ariel snapped back.

"I see." He nodded. "Then you're going to handle our business for both of the shops?"

"Business? It's called extortion."

His smile widened. "Protection," he corrected her.

Chapter Two

At five the next morning Pete faced an inevitable fact of life. He'd lived a soft life in New York for too long. Busy with his career, he'd taken time only for a morning jog. The quick excuse for exercise didn't compare to the good old days, when he'd spent weekends mountain climbing.

As he finished a racquetball game with an old friend, Bill Kunutz, Pete ached everywhere.

Strolling out of the health club with Bill, known as "Nutzy" in college, Pete displayed enormous self-control. Somehow he resisted the urge to grimace at the hamstring tightening in his right leg and refrained from calling his friend by the ridiculous nickname even though Bill was doing a superb job of razzing Pete about being out of shape.

As they walked toward their cars, Bill rambled, raving about his twin sons, informing Pete that the best place to eat in the city was at the Hillcrest—his restaurant—and reminiscing about mutual acquaintances.

"Wessell. Jonathan Wessell," Bill went on, reaching into his pants' pocket for his car keys. "You remember him. He was the last person I expected Ariel to go out with. A banker's son. The guy always looked as if he was sniffing the air and didn't like it."

Pete remembered him. More than once Pete had noticed Wessell eyeing Ariel during a literature class. Because she'd never even glanced his way, Pete had been stunned when his father had written that Ariel had married Wessell and moved to California with him.

"I don't know what she saw in him," Bill added.

Pete jingled the car keys in his hand. "Smarts."

"We all were," Bill returned, exhibiting the same cockiness that he'd been famous for in college.

"Money."

"I'd believe that about any woman but Ariel," Bill insisted. "She's too much of an earth child to let money motivate her. And Wessell always made me think of an English butler. Very proper all the time." Bill eyed Pete. "I think she rebounded because of you. Went from bad to worse."

Pete laughed. "Thanks a lot, buddy."

Bill leaned his upper body toward Pete as if anticipating an exchange of government secrets. "Tell me now why you did something so stupid as breaking up with her. Did they give you a lobotomy in New York?"

Pete stepped up to his Mazda.

"Two years is a hell of a long time to be with one woman and then dump her."

"I didn't dump her."

Bill responded to the fierce sharpness in Pete's voice and took a step back. "Sorry, Pete. But hell, I thought..."

Everyone expected you two... Well, we thought you were going to New York to settle in and then you'd come back to marry her. Guess it didn't work out."

Pete shook his head. "No, it didn't work out that way."

"Plenty of pretty ladies in New York to choose from. Right?"

Pete gave him a semblance of a smile. "Plenty." He pushed back his cuff and looked at his watch. He had a morning filled with appointments. But by noon he'd have time to visit Virginia.

Bill poked a finger at the air as if pinpointing a spot on a calendar. "I'll meet you on the court Friday morning," he added as he continued walking toward his car. "Five-thirty," Bill yelled out.

Pete nodded. "Okay." He grinned back at Bill. "And get in shape."

Bill guffawed loudly. "Me! You, man. You're living proof that athletes can go soft."

"People change," Pete said good-naturedly as he opened the door to his RX-7. People do change, he reflected. From everything he'd heard about Ariel, she'd changed, too. One thing hadn't: he'd never stopped caring about her.

Ariel bagged the red silk umbrella for a customer and managed a smile and a thank-you, but she glanced nervously at the clock.

The day after the window had been broken, the crate of gourds, stolen over a week ago, had been returned. Smashed to pieces. The note had stated "I'll be back."

Yesterday, Siske, the raspy-voiced, barrel-shaped man with the sneering smile, had informed her that he would call her again to make arrangements for the collection of the insurance premium. Ariel had nearly laughed in his face when he'd used that term. Nearly laughed.

What she'd really been was frightened.

She shifted her gaze to the door's cracked window. Siske had pointed to it and told her that the damage was notification of a premium due. Paying him had never entered her mind. Threats always had failed to motivate her. If anything, she rebelled against them.

Jonathan's repeated threats of divorce were the result of her refusal to "shape up." In his mind, "shape up" had meant "conform." A banker's wife wasn't supposed to resemble a flower child's Gypsy sister or someone reliving her adolescence in jeans and sneakers. His threats had failed to reform her into a conservative fashion plate.

And Siske's threat infuriated her.

She'd stalled on informing the police. She knew that letting them handle him was the most logical thing to do, but Siske's threat had included her mother's flower shop. Reluctantly, Ariel might risk her own business, but for days she'd pondered her right to risk her mother's.

Nervous, she jumped at the sound of the door opening. With her peripheral vision Ariel caught sight of a man. She prayed that he was a customer and not Siske, and tensed even before she turned around. She caught a glimpse of a youthful face, but all her attention centered on the flower box in the delivery boy's hands.

Pete frowned at the Closed sign on the door of Ginnie's Bouquets. What kind of businesswoman closed her store on a Monday at eleven o'clock?

He spun away from the door, but his stride faltered as he eyed the monstrosity in the adjacent store's display window. An oxidized copper elephant's head the size of a sofa end table took center stage. Situated around it were a marble chess set and a hand-painted sake set. Wood and papier-mâché marionettes from Burma hung in the upper corners of the window.

Pete stepped toward the door of the store to peer through its window. For a long moment he stared at the bent head of the woman who fussed with a vase of yellow daffodils, then he reached for the doorknob.

At the soft click of the door Ariel slowly raised her head and parted the flowers, hoping not to find herself standing face-to-face with Siske's disgusting sneer.

Instead, Pete grinned back at her.

Overcome by a sudden confusion, she rocked back on her heels. Her defenses had gathered force through the years to protect her. She dodged the effect of his grin, telling herself it didn't charm her. It didn't excite her. It didn't turn her legs to a substance as wobbly as Jell-O.

If only he hadn't smiled, she thought. The too familiar grin sparked memories of nights filled with loving whispers and soft caresses. She remembered all of them.

She remembered, too, how he'd looked in the soft light of morning, when his hair had been tousled and his eyes hooded and filled with passion.

She remembered all the vulnerability, all the hopes, all the love as the intervening years seemed to disappear.

"Browsing or shopping?" she finally asked, trying for a cool tone, but her voice sounded as breathless as if she'd run several blocks.

Pete had to work hard at hiding his amusement. Any other woman would have said hello first, pretended surprise at seeing him, asked how he'd been. She was as unpredictable as ever. "I haven't decided."

Nothing was worse, Ariel decided, than two people who'd once been intimate trying to act like acquaintances. She'd keep the conversation casual and calm, even though she felt as if someone were strangling her. Later she'd scream. Or cry. Or collapse. "I'd heard that you moved back here."

"The Evan-to-Virginia grapevine?"

"Yes."

"The company moved me here to open a branch office," he answered distractedly while skimming the store. Imported woven baskets, hand-decorated paper fans, and colorful silk umbrellas hung from the ceiling. Behind a counter were hand-painted masks from Burma, wood inlay depictions of the Italian Riviera, and mother-of-pearl ducks from Pakistan. Shelves of glass and dishware from Italy and France and Spain led to a display area of small straw huts. Hung on the outside were oversized baskets filled with colorful miniature batik and wheat straw baskets. Another hut created a backdrop for hand-carved African masks.

Pete scanned shelves of copper and brass goblets and pitchers, hand-painted Japanese vases, and counters of Australian soap.

Ariel watched him until his gaze swung back to her. "You're still with Bryant and Bryant?" At his nod, she added, "Good old B and B." Instantly she regretted the harshness in her tone. It revealed too much to him, but an old bitter memory was stirred every time she heard that company's name. During Pete's last evening with her, he'd said Bryant and Bryant at least a half dozen times.

"Bryant and Bryant wants me in New York."

"Bryant and Bryant is a conservative firm."

"Bryant and Bryant wouldn't understand if I had a live-in. We'll have to wait."

Until when? she'd wanted to ask. But he'd stared at her, saying nothing else, and she'd known then that the goodbye was final.

"I like your store," he said now.

Ariel nodded a thank-you.

Her hair hung longer and wilder around her face, Pete noted. Her body seemed slimmer. As she shoved her fingers into the pockets of her tight jeans, his gaze traveled down her legs to the tops of the boots, where her jeans were neatly tucked. She was slenderer than before, but her skin looked as soft as he remembered, and he so ached to touch her that his stomach knotted. Then his eyes locked with hers. The blue was darker, harboring her wariness.

Uneasy, Pete stepped around a carved stone statue and bent forward to read the card attached to the llama. "Indonesia."

Ariel released an exaggerated sigh that pulled his gaze back to her. "Are you looking for something in particular?"

Pete straightened. Her question was loaded. He sensed he was looking for something that he'd have to search long and hard to find. New York had its share of beautiful women, but she was the one who'd inched her way under his skin, burrowed herself so deeply into him that his mind refused to banish memories of the love and passion he'd once felt for her. With his head he gestured toward the yellow daffodils. "Did they just arrive?"

"This bouquet did." As he moved closer she felt herself quiver. In an attempt to combat the sensation, she turned away and set the vase of daffodils on a nearby counter, but she kept him in her line of vision.

He paused beside the shelf of stemware and reached for a champagne glass. "I'm glad to see that you didn't toss them in the garbage."

"My mother is a florist," Ariel returned in a light tone that contradicted the tenseness coiling around her. "That would be sacrilegious." Instinctively, unwittingly, she smiled. She'd never mastered feigned coolness because she'd always thought anger a futile emotion, a waste of time. Though she didn't want to, her natural warmth prevented her from reacting in any way but a friendly one.

If she'd yelled or swung at him, Pete was thinking, she would have had less impact on him. He'd forgotten the incredible warmth of her smile. He'd met sophisticated women who had elegant manners and wore designer clothes. They were like caviar and symphonies to him. Ariel was like cotton candy and carnivals and a warm summer day. She was a stunner.

Ariel leaned back against a counter and eyed him. She'd been shocked by his sudden appearance, and though certain that she hadn't paled or revealed her true feelings to him, she couldn't ignore how quickly and easily he'd sent her pulse racing.

"I came to see your mother. Her store isn't open," he said.

Ariel shook her head. "No. On Sundays and Mondays it's closed."

Again he looked around him. "Have you been here long? I'd heard that you'd moved to California."

"I was there for three years."

He noted that her voice was soft and not quite steady.

"What else did you learn?" she asked.

"I heard about your divorce."

Ariel said nothing. What could she say? *You left and I looked for another. He wasn't you.*

The silence hung in the air, each passing second ticking away as if marking all the years that had passed since they'd parted.

"Should I say I'm sorry?" he asked at last.

He looked so perplexed that she laughed. "Bite your tongue."

A quick, familiar grin sprang to his face, nearly undoing her. He turned away from a set of crystal stemware and approached her. "About your mother and my father," he started. "I'm assuming that you know they're..."

"Lovers."

"Are they?"

"Of course they are."

"My father and your mother?"

"Pete, I'm aware of the relationship."

"They're having an affair?"

His astonishment amused her. "Why are you surprised?"

"My father is fifty-seven."

"So? Is he supposed to turn sexless after fifty? Do you plan to?"

He felt himself turn red. It was a first for him and would rank high on his list of the dumbest things he'd ever done, he decided.

She observed his obvious annoyance with himself.

He gave his head a slow shake. "I don't know." Good-naturedly, he laughed at himself. "I didn't think. I guess I'd hoped it wasn't that serious. If they're making love, then..." He shrugged. "I suppose marriage is inevitable."

"Not always," she pointedly reminded him.

"Ariel..."

She resisted the sudden softness in his voice. "Some men marry their jobs."

"Just a minute." His voice rose defensively.

She whirled away and rounded the high counter. "Nice seeing you again," she announced while bending over to unpack a carton.

Her subtle message didn't faze him. At that moment he faced truth; he faced himself. For years he'd fed himself nonsense about her, believed he no longer cared about her. It was drivel, pure and simple. "I'm not leaving yet."

Startled by his voice close behind her, she whipped a look over her shoulder at him. He stood firm, straight-backed, arrogantly tall, from his highly polished shoes to the top of his dark head. She faced him squarely. "You always pushed."

"Still do."

"So I see."

"We need to talk."

"I'm busy, Pete."

Out of habit, he spoke with authority in his voice. "We need to talk," he insisted, taking the sculptured dove from her hand.

He saw that her eyes snapped with fiery annoyance. She'd always made him think of heat. He'd assumed it was because of her red hair, but it was her eyes. They bore the intensity of a blue blaze when her anger stirred.

"Years ago you said enough to last me a lifetime," she told him.

"I don't want to talk about us."

Ariel frowned.

"We need to talk about our parents. Or are you pleased about what seems to be happening?"

"Lord, no. Your father is totally wrong for my mother."

"No more so than your mother is wrong for my dad."

"What's wrong with my mother?"

"She's beautiful, with a kind heart and a sweetness few women half her age possess. But she has an adolescent symptom that is rarely studied in geriatrics."

"Quit the mumbo jumbo."

"Some people might say she fits the description of a flake."

Her eyes narrowed dangerously. "You mean she knows how to have fun. And forty-nine is too young to be studied by doctors in the field of geriatrics."

"Your mother is forty-nine?"

"Fifty—fifty-five," she responded, unable to echo her mother's white lie to Evan. "And if you think that's so old, what did you do for your thirtieth birthday? Send yourself a black wreath?"

"I got drunk," Pete admitted. "Soused. And had a hangover the next day that made me feel as if I were eighty with one leg in the grave."

"Serves you right," she replied, but couldn't help smiling. She knew he wasn't as disapproving of her mother as he sounded. His sharp comments stemmed more from worry than from dislike. "When I turn thirty, I'm going to throw myself an enormous bash and make an announcement to the world."

He watched her eyes, caught up in their sparkle. "What announcement?" he asked.

"Look out, world—" she grinned impishly "—here I come."

She hadn't changed. And he was glad she hadn't. She was sunshine. Warmth. She breezed into a room and turned on the lights. He'd never known anything or anyone to dampen her mood for long. Who knew her better than he? He'd lived with her; he'd seen her smiles and heard her laughter daily. He'd witnessed those rare serious moments, but they had fled swiftly. She enjoyed life to its fullest. And disturbingly, he was beginning to realize just how much he'd missed enjoying it with her.

"Why was your thirtieth birthday such a mournful time?" she asked.

He picked up a snowfall paperweight on the counter. Briefly he shook it and watched the white flakes float around in their enclosure. "I didn't accomplish everything I'd hoped to do."

"So what?"

"Some people plan their lives beyond the minute, Ariel."

"Plans can be rewritten."

"Then goals aren't met."

She rolled her eyes, making him aware of how pompous he sounded.

They still viewed life through different lenses, he mused. What if they had married? He could easily visualize them entertaining J.C. Bryant at their house, a home decorated with a hodgepodge collection of whatever had grabbed Ariel's fancy.

Pete eyed a wall hanging that consisted of bones and string. Some African fertility symbol, probably. A hanging like that on his living room wall would have made the steely-eyed J.C. Bryant, in his banker's gray suit, swallow his dentures. And from that moment on J.C. would have kept a watchful eye on Pete, expecting him to abscond with some corporation's funds and fly to Fiji with his fun-loving wife.

Grabbing the Closed sign from under the cash register, Ariel became aware of his sudden silence. Instinctively she responded to his troubled frown and touched his forearm in a reassuring manner. "You have a lot of time left to do things." She felt his muscle tense beneath her fingertips and withdrew her hand quickly. She shouldn't have touched him.

For an eternity of a second she nearly forgot a vital fact. Distance. She would never let him hurt her again, and with a touch she'd nearly forgotten that. She started to step back but his hand slid over hers like an undulating snake and his fingers curled on her wrist, halting her movement.

Pete kept a firm grip on her wrist. She was small, like her mother. Five-feet-two. But the top of her head came to the bridge of his nose. "You've grown."

A smile danced in his eyes, Ariel saw. She stared at him as if he were crazy.

"You've grown," he repeated. "You weren't this tall before."

As she looked down he followed her gaze to her feet and the high heels of her knee-high laced boots. "Oh."

They laughed together, then their eyes met. For a second the intervening years disappeared. For a second she stood close to the man who'd changed her from a young girl to a woman, the man who'd shared the wonders of loving with her, the man whom she'd wanted to spend the rest of her life with.

Fighting an overwhelming urge to stay near him, she stepped back, moving an arm's length away before he uncurled his fingers from her wrist.

Pete watched as she shifted her gaze from his. With any other woman he'd consider that a victory of sorts. Not her. She had not looked away in confusion. Rather, she suddenly seemed more concerned with the clock than with him. As a small line creased her brow he sensed her deep desire—not for him, but to get rid of him.

"It's nearly lunchtime," Ariel said. "Do you want to get something to eat? We can talk then."

Perplexed now, he would've sworn she wanted him to leave. He shook his head, realizing she confused him as much now as she always had. "Lunch is fine with me," he answered, noting again her preoccupation with the clock.

Ariel grabbed her purse from under the counter. She decided she would spend a half hour at the restaurant with him, then leave him there. She wouldn't return to the store; Siske might call or be waiting for her, and she didn't want another confrontation with him yet. From the restaurant she'd catch a bus instead of getting her car. With any luck she'd get the problem into the hands of a professional without Pete's knowing about it, and Siske wouldn't have visited her shop yet.

With any luck.

She stared at the top of Pete's dark head as he bent and inspected a napkin holder, grimacing.

"What is this?" he asked, holding it out to her.

At her answer he frowned at the object in his hand. "Why would anyone want a crossbones and skull on a napkin holder?"

"For a Caribbean pirate's party."

Pete laughed. "Why?"

"Why not?"

"Why did I ask?" he said lightly, and opened the door for her.

She walked at a clipped pace. Others might view the stride as contrary to her easygoing, breezy manner, but if Ariel wanted something, she barreled ahead full blast to get it, using charm and smiles and an intelligence that outwitted any unsuspecting person who stood in her way. Because he knew all that, Pete pondered her lunch invitation and realized that she'd deliberately whisked him out of the shop. Why remained a mystery to him.

As Ariel made a sharp right turn into a restaurant, Pete followed. He paused in the doorway, watching her wind a quick path around tables to a booth in a far corner. He should have stopped her before she'd made her way so far into the restaurant. He should have paid attention to where they were going. Instead he'd been thinking about her.

He'd been letting the fragrance of her perfume drift over him. He'd been allowing masculine responses to an extremely feminine, beautiful woman dominate his usual logical thought processes.

With a resigned shrug he made his way to where she was sitting. If he didn't stop daydreaming while he was with her, she'd sell him the London Bridge and convince him it was still in England.

Seating himself across from her, he eyed the luncheon special posted behind the counter. Seaweed soup. "Unusual place," he remarked.

"I love the food here." Ariel watched him tighten his jaw. He obviously hated it. *Good*, she thought. She'd deliberately chosen the health food restaurant, aware he'd prefer a hamburger or roast beef sandwich for lunch. With any luck he'd poke at the dish, end their discussion quickly, and she could leave to take care of Siske.

Pete shifted on the molded plastic booth seat. *Make the best of it*, he told himself, refusing to give her that edge. He grabbed the menu and hunted through the list for something that sounded as if it might contain meat.

"Try the—" she began.

"I've already made a decision."

"Fine."

"Do they sprinkle arsenic on it at a companion's request?"

She peered at him over the top of her menu. "Do you think I'd do that?"

"No." He let his gaze wander around the room. "Slow torture is more your style."

Ariel hid a smile behind the menu. She'd forgotten how good a sport he could be.

While she ordered the chili, he wavered between two choices. He hated not knowing what to expect. Neither of the names hinted at the ingredients in the dish. He made a stab at being adventurous and placed an order for Green Delight.

The moment the waitress walked away and he saw Ariel's grin, he knew he'd made a mistake. "What is it?"

"Why didn't you ask before ordering it?"

He heaved a sigh, then admitted, "Pride. I didn't want to give you the satisfaction. What is it?"

"One of your favorites."

Her airy tone forewarned him. "Not spinach?"

Ariel wagged her head.

"Zucchini?"

She smiled.

Narrowing one eye at her, he asked hopefully, "Like fried zucchini?"

"'Fraid not," she responded a little too brightly.

"I should have eaten a bigger breakfast."

"You rarely ate breakfast. All you ever did was inhale caffeine."

"If I'm going to have more lunches with you, I may change my habits," he remarked wryly.

"You aren't."

"Don't be so quick with that answer."

She straightened her back. "We're here to discuss our parents. That's all."

A door couldn't have slammed harder in his face, but it only made him more determined to open it again and keep it that way, he realized, reaching for his iced tea.

Ariel softened her tone. "We both agree that they could be making a mistake."

Pete set down the glass. "They will be." He raised his hands in a helpless gesture. "Ariel, they're wrong for each other. They don't have any common interests."

She leaned back with a puzzled expression. "You've been away. How do you know that?"

"Do you think they have?"

Ariel couldn't really say. Her mother had offered her a rare gift when Ariel had turned twenty-one: she minded her own business. For that reason Ariel had returned the favor. "I wasn't even aware they were dating until a month ago."

"How long have you been back?"

"Six months."

"And your divorce?"

"We weren't married very long. And we'd stopped living together nearly two years ago. I stayed in California for a while," she explained. "I was working as a receptionist in a doctor's office." She watched as what resembled a skeptical smirk flickered across his face. "Why that look?"

"Such a sedate atmosphere doesn't suit you."

"It was a pediatrician. I gave out balloons and smiley-face coloring books in between answering the phone."

His smile widened.

"Does that sound more believable?" she asked.

"Yes. Why didn't you stay?"

"I had a degree in merchandising but couldn't find a job," she answered simply, wondering why they kept getting sidetracked from their discussion. "According to my mother, she and Evan have been dating five months."

"And you never knew?"

"Pete, I don't ask her about her love life. And she doesn't ask me about mine."

"So there have been men since your divorce?"

"Obviously your father didn't confide in you before this, either," she said, ignoring his question.

"No. I didn't know he was even dating Virginia until yesterday."

"Then why are you so convinced they have nothing in common?"

"Do they?"

Ariel looked at the bowl of chili placed before her. "I can't imagine what. My mother likes ragtime."

"My father likes Bach."

"My mother likes to dance."

"My father likes to read."

Affection warmed her voice. "My mother loves Oriental food."

"I remember." Pete grinned. "Does she still wear that geisha outfit while serving it?"

"Her Madame Butterfly costume? Oh, yes. And she dresses up as Carmen whenever she serves *chimichangas*. And she has a Hawaiian skirt and several leis for the nights when she serves her Polynesian spare ribs."

Pete poked a fork at a mound of bean sprouts, then shoved them to the side, praying something else was beneath them on his plate. He found a green mound and stuck the fork into it. "My father likes liver and onions."

"Do you?"

"I hate that. But it would be a feast right now," he mumbled as he cautiously sampled the green concoction.

Noticing him eyeing her bread, she handed it to him. "Seven different grains."

He accepted it without hesitation and motioned with his fork. "Do you want your hard-boiled egg?"

Ariel laughed and slipped it onto his plate. "Anything else?"

"The carrot curl."

She reached forward and exchanged plates with him. "Here. We'll trade. Mine is chili."

His hand covered hers, stopping her action. "You don't have to."

"Oh, but I do," she said laughingly. "You look in agony."

"How could this be chili? No meat."

"Soybean."

He winced.

"Listen to me this time. It's good."

As she wiggled her fingers beneath his hand, Pete held firm. "Will you listen to me, too?"

She scowled at him.

"We could be seeing a lot more of each other than we ever expected," Pete said, acting as if she would agree gladly to his request.

She should have known it wouldn't be easy seeing him again. "Yes, we might."

He watched her incline her head skeptically. It was a thoughtful look, a familiar gesture to him, one he'd seen before when she was worrying about something. His gut tightened, and he softened his voice, suddenly not feeling quite so sure of himself. "It's been a lot of years, Ariel. What's the point of remembering the bad times?"

Ariel drew a long, hard breath. "You ask a lot after what you made clear to me years ago."

"What do you think I made clear?"

"That you enjoyed being with me."

"That's true," he said softly.

"That making love was very good between us."

He nodded, hating the pressure building within his chest.

"That I wasn't quite suitable to be your wife."

"Oh, damn, Ariel." He looked away.

One emotion ran high between them—vulnerability, Ariel thought. She tensed, afraid if she gave in to it, then he'd be back in her life again. "After you left, I made a dreadful mistake, Pete. I married on the rebound. I married a man very much like you."

"Wessell?"

"He was a substitute," she said honestly.

"For me?"

"Yes." She ran a fingertip down the cold, wet glass of iced tea. "But before your ego blows up all out of proportion, let me tell you that he did make me miserable." She met his eyes. "As you would have."

"You don't pull any punches, do you, Ariel?"

"You never did."

"Are you getting even with me for—"

"No," she answered, and smiled.

He believed she wasn't. She was stating the truth. Unfortunately she could be painfully truthful sometimes, but game-playing had never suited her.

"You made the right decision, Pete. But then you always did think things out more thoroughly than I did. And we probably are going to see a great deal of each other if Evan proposes to my mother. That's why I decided that we should clear the air now."

"Get both of us on the right track?"

"Yes, something like that. And..." She paused, then added, "Call a truce."

"Okay." He nodded. "But one thing."

Ariel met his gaze.

"I'm not sure I made the right decision four years ago."

Damn him. Ariel stomped across the street, furious with him for having hinted that he might have made a mistake when he'd left her. Past mistakes sometimes couldn't be forgotten. Why had it taken him so long to consider that? Why had he placed his work ahead of her? Why hadn't he come back years ago?

She didn't need him back in her life. Nothing had changed. No, that wasn't true. Everything had changed. Jonathan had taught her how wrong she was for men like Pete.

They cared about what other people thought. They liked predictability. She was never predictable. Predictable was boring.

She and Pete wouldn't have been happy together because she couldn't be the kind of woman he needed. And she shouldn't be thinking about how damn good he'd looked to her or the sexy grin that sprang to his face. She had to think about another man with a sneering grin who meant immediate trouble.

Pete stood outside the restaurant and watched her stride quickly away from him. She'd started to respond, then had glanced at the clock and darted from the restaurant without saying more than a goodbye.

Pete frowned as she ran down the sidewalk to catch a bus. What was she doing? Where was she going in such a hurry? He'd assumed she'd planned on returning to the store. Instead she was headed in the opposite direction.

Something was wrong, and he sensed that this time it had nothing to do with him.

Chapter Three

Evan shrugged out of his tweed sport coat and settled on Virginia's sofa, with its safari design of lion and giraffe heads. "I talked to Pete yesterday," he said.

Virginia whirled around, the cocoon-style jacket of her white jumpsuit flying open like butterfly's wings. She leaned forward across the futuristic smoked-glass coffee table and handed Evan a drink decorated with a cherry, an orange slice, and a bright miniature umbrella. "You should have brought him to dinner."

Evan eyed the yellow liquid in the glass. "Ginnie, what is this?"

"A Banana Slammer."

He peered over the top of his glasses at the bright-faced, smiling woman. "And what is that?"

"Take a sip," she urged. "Then I'll tell you."

He bent his gray head and complied. Cautiously. "Hmm. Banana and . . . ?"

"Vodka, a touch of grenadine, and a squirt of pine-apple," she called out, rushing back to the kitchen.

He chuckled. "It's very good."

She stood in the arched doorway, her trim figure sil-houetted by the glow of the kitchen's soft blue light. Bearing a plate of appetizers, she passed the stereo and flicked a switch. The soft strains of a Bach violin con-certo drifted from the dual speakers.

"Why didn't you bring him to dinner?" she asked.

"Peter," Evan said, resting an arm on the back of the sofa behind her as she settled beside him, "may be a problem child for the first time in his life." At Ginnie's quizzical look, he went on. "He never gave me the usual problems while he was growing up."

"A sensible boy, you had said."

"Yes, he was. He graduated with top honors from high school and college, won trophies playing college base-ball and was never the sullen, uncommunicative teen-ager."

"An overachiever."

Evan ran his fingertips lightly over the top of Ginnie's arm. "Hardworking, ambitious, conscientious."

"Of all of Ariel's boyfriends, he was my favorite. So bright. And he looked at Ariel with such love." Her smile slipped. "I do wish that he'd been the one she'd married instead of Jonathan."

"That was Peter's fault, you know."

"Of course. Ariel never stopped loving him."

Her simplistic observation prompted him to hug her more tightly to him. "I'd have expected you to have un-pleasant thoughts about him after that."

"Oh, never," Virginia assured him. "Some men need more time than others to learn what's really important."

"I'm not sure Peter has yet."

"He will, dear. He will."

Evan sipped more of his drink. "Does Ariel hate him?"

"Of course not, but she has a stubborn streak. She was a difficult child," Ginnie informed him. "She still can be. She's very hardheaded. Independent. Strong-willed."

Evan made his own observation. "Loving."

"Yes. Yes, she is. And once she loves someone, that feeling never leaves her. She still loves him."

Her resolve that she felt certain about this matter was reflected in her eyes, Evan noted.

"She doesn't want to admit that. But she will someday."

"You sound so sure."

"Evan, she's my daughter."

He laughed. "Amazing."

"What is?"

"Your belief in everything always working out."

"It must. When something is right, it's right." She touched his thigh affectionately. "The youth always think they know more than everyone else. But they need more time than we do to see things clearly."

He glanced at the bookshelf. The works of Thoreau and Emerson dominated the shelves. "Seeing clearly is definitely not one of Peter's greatest traits."

"Give him time."

"I'm willing. But as I told you, he might prove to be a problem for us."

She cast him a quizzical look.

"He's suddenly developed an annoying trait—meddlesomeness."

Ginnie leaned back and rested her head on his shoulder. "Oh, dear. He's not pleased that you're seeing me?"

Evan bent his head toward hers and kissed her temple. "He needs to get used to the idea."

Ginnie sighed heavily. "Unfortunately, Evan, my daughter seems to have a similar problem."

"It's to be expected."

She raised her face to him and smiled. "Yes. Children always have problems perceiving their parents accurately."

"My son sees me as a stodgy, straitlaced man who gave up some of life's basic needs a decade ago."

"My daughter believes I need a keeper."

Evan exchanged a smile with her. "To prevent you from doing something outrageous?"

"Can you imagine? I don't know where she developed such notions about me." Her giggle rippled in the air. "Perhaps we need to straighten them out."

Evan inclined his head to see her face better. "Ginnie, what are you—"

"I have a splendid idea."

He frowned dubiously. "Sweetheart, occasionally your splendid ideas are overwhelming."

Ginnie laughed. "This one is." She pressed close against him. "Want to hear it?"

"Perhaps later," Evan murmured as her warm body distracted him.

"While they're making up their minds about us, why don't we nudge them back together?"

His head reared back. "Oh, Ginnie, I don't know."

"Trust me. Everything will work out perfectly."

"But . . ."

She coiled an arm around his neck and brushed her lips against his as she slipped off his glasses. "Don't you think it's a splendid idea?"

"Actually—" he nuzzled her neck and laughed "—all of your ideas are splendid," he admitted, pulling her closer.

What was Ariel doing at a police station? Pete stood under the overhang near the stationhouse door. The sky had turned a slate gray during the past few hours. His mood was dismal.

He felt foolish standing outside a police station. So why was he here? Because Ariel was. With her usual flair, she had complicated his life without much effort. He should have gone to his office. Instead he was hanging around the station house like some stool pigeon who was waiting for his contact.

He shouldn't get involved. She wouldn't want him to. She had her life; he had his.

Every quality that made her the wrong kind of woman for Peter Turner, junior consultant at Bryant and Bryant, enticed him. Her quick laugh, her straightforward manner, her announcements that something hideous was lovely, her unself-conscious interest in any person, even the bum on the street, sent his adrenaline pumping.

When he was with her, even when she was arguing with him, he felt lighthearted. He always felt more alive.

She was the breath of the wind, the heat of the sun, the restless flow of the ocean. She was torrential; she was calm. She was like a bursting blossom at springtime. She was never dull. Never predictable. Never wishy-washy.

A Bryant and Bryant consultant needed a wife who dressed conservatively, chose Chippendale chairs, didn't make waves, kept her opinions to herself, and avoided having a reason to visit a police station.

That would never be Ariel.

Pete jammed a hand into his pants' pocket and swore at himself. He shouldn't get involved. He should leave. Hell! Unless he could locate a switch to flick off what he felt for her, he couldn't avoid getting involved.

He leaned against the wall of the stucco building and watched raindrops splash on the sidewalk before him. Trailing her went against everything he believed in, but when she'd rushed from the restaurant and caught a bus that took her in the opposite direction of her shop, his curiosity had sent him racing for his car.

If he was so damned curious, why didn't he go in and find out why she was there? Because it was none of his business. He'd set down that rule years before, and she seemed determined to remind him of that mistake. But even income tax auditors were occasionally sympathetic to human mistakes, Pete reflected.

Ariel shifted on the chair across the desk from the police sergeant.

"All you know is that he calls himself Siske?" the sergeant asked.

Ariel nodded. She'd spent nearly half an hour sitting in the outer office, waiting to see someone. Then she'd presented her problem to a woman who had seemed more interested in Ariel's earrings. Becoming exasperated, Ariel had been ready to rip the matching silver-plated lizards from her ears and present them to the woman.

When the woman had finally ushered Ariel into the sergeant's office, he'd given her an equally funny look. For the next few moments the discussion had focused on her name.

"Ariel is an unusual name," he commented.

"My mother loves Shakespeare."

His eyes had registered that he wasn't making any connection.

"Ariel was the airy spirit in *The Tempest*."

He'd merely nodded. "Different, Ms. Hammond."

Ariel had thanked him, deciding to accept his comment as a compliment. Now he seemed just as taken with the name Siske.

"You're absolutely sure that his name is Siske?"

"He seemed proud to announce it."

As he folded his arms across his enormous chest, a corner of the sergeant's lips curled. "He would. He's arrogant enough to tell his name."

"I did think that odd. Why would he identify himself to me?"

The sergeant swiveled his chair away from his desk. "Because he's sure that you wouldn't go to the police. He makes himself known to the shop owners, feeling secure that anyone he tells his name to will be too frightened to contact us."

Ariel frowned. "You sound as if you know him."

"Siske is the muscle man for a known extortion ring."

Ariel slumped back on the chair. "Then he means business."

"Serious business."

"He—well, I believe he was the one who broke the window of my shop's door and stole the crate of gourds."

"Gentle touches."

Ariel tensed. "They were?"

"His tactics usually are more demonstrative."

"Am I in danger?"

"If you weren't going to pay him, you would be."

"I'm not," Ariel said firmly.

The sergeant smiled, deep lines forming at the corners of his eyes. "Then it's wise that you came to us."

"I don't understand. If you know that this man is a criminal, why isn't he arrested?"

"Because no one has come forward to point the finger at him. Until you."

"I'm the only one?"

He nodded slowly. "We have a good idea that he's already getting payments from several other shop owners, but no one else has complained."

"His threat included my mother's store. She has the flower shop next to mine."

He swiveled his chair back and wrote across a sheet of paper as Ariel gave him the name and address of her mother's store.

"Has he contacted her?"

Ariel shook her head. Nervously she ran a sweaty palm over a jean-clad thigh. "He assumes I'll handle the payment for both our stores. My mother isn't even aware of the threat."

"You didn't tell her?"

"No." Ariel inched forward on her chair in a conspiratorial manner. "My mother... You see, I thought it would be best if I took care of this problem. So I'd appreciate it if you didn't tell her."

He studied her closely. "Does she have a heart condition or some other life-threatening problem?"

"No." Ariel blew out a long breath. Describing her mother to most people wasn't easy. "My mother would probably dump a vase on his head."

A flicker of a smile curved the edges of the sergeant's lips. "Feisty."

"She's occasionally impulsive," Ariel offered.

One of his heavy brows lifted slightly. "Like when she named you?"

Ariel laughed, not at all offended by his comment. More than one person had remarked about her unusual name. "Yes. She was reading *The Tempest* in the hospital." She raised her hands in the air. "And so Ariel was born."

He laughed silently, his shoulders shaking. "Perhaps for now it would be best that you keep this between us. I'll have an officer pass your store regularly and watch it. And after I talk to my superior, I'll contact you about what we believe is the best way to handle this."

"And if Siske returns? He promised to contact me soon," Ariel reminded him anxiously. "What do I do then?"

He raised a hand and scratched the back of his head. "Tell him that you don't have all the money for him yet. But you'll have it for him soon. Try to give us as much time as you think you can without placing yourself in danger."

Ariel nodded and stood. Her legs felt rubbery. She might put on a brave act for everyone, but Siske scared the daylights out of her. "Thank you, Sergeant..." She glanced down at the nameplate on his desk. "Detective Hernandez."

"We'll be in touch," he assured her. "Don't you worry."

Ariel offered a slip of a smile. As he stood to shake her hand she noted that he was over six feet three. Nothing was more reassuring than to have Arnold Schwarzenegger's replica standing in her corner.

The click of her boot heels on the tile floor echoed through the hall as she strode toward the exit. Her lone footsteps emphasized how she felt at the moment. She wished there was someone close she could share the problem with. She couldn't tell her mother. As much as

Ariel loved her, Virginia tended toward harebrained ideas. And to share the information with anyone else might place that person in danger, too. Other than the police, no one could help her with this problem. It was hers alone.

As she flung open the door, she paused. The sight of Pete's broad back played havoc with her emotions at the moment. She needed someone, so who was she fooling? She needed him. If things were different between them...but they weren't.

Mentally she geared herself for the next few moments. Anger promised the easiest path, she decided, fuming that he'd followed her. He had no right to push himself back into her life. He'd chosen to leave it years ago. She struggled to hold on to those feelings while she was plagued by others. Her emotions seesawed and her mind filled with the kinds of thoughts youthful fantasizers thrived on. Did he care about her? Did he wish they hadn't ever broken up?

Pride took control as she stepped closer to him. He hadn't cared enough before. Why should he now?

She squared her shoulders and listened to the rain pounding on the pavement. Rain had pattered against the windows during the first time they'd made love in his apartment.

Thunder had muffled their moans while she'd learned of the exquisite pleasure of a man's touch. She'd loved the intimacy, marveled at the rough texture of his skin beneath her hands. She'd opened more than her body to him that day. As he'd filled her with his warmth, more than her flesh had blended with his. She'd relinquished all the love she would ever have for any man. Every time after that, he'd taken possession of more of it, until she no longer could offer such deep feelings to any other.

When the door clicked behind her, his head swiveled in her direction. His eyes met hers, and she felt swept back in time. She would never ask, but she was certain that the sight of rain had strayed his thoughts to those moments and others when the headiness of lovemaking had enveloped them. She struggled for a breath, feeling as if the wind had been knocked out of her. "Did you follow me?"

"Obviously."

"Why?" She mustered indignation. "What right...?"

"No right."

"Then why?"

"If I knew, I might not be here."

His confusion came through clearly in his voice. Ariel steeled herself, sensing that a softness, any compassion for his feelings at the moment, might sway her into his arms.

She stepped away from the doorway and stared out at the rain. Taking control of uncomfortable situations worked best for her. She decided against a challenge and sniffed exaggeratedly. "The rain smells good."

"Why were you in there?"

"I needed to talk to someone," she answered, deciding that wasn't a lie.

"To whom?"

She raised a smile to him. Pete understood what she was doing. Not all of her smiles mean the same thing. This wasn't the warm one. Cool, it announced her wintry thoughts. Without her saying a word, she delivered a message—*Mind your own business.*

"A friend," Ariel offered as an answer. Detective Hernandez was that, she reflected—in a broad sense of the word, anyway. Weren't the police always going around to schoolrooms with their "We're your friends" campaign?

He stared at her for a long time, considering her manner. He more than anyone appreciated the strength of her stubbornness. As her foot moved onto a step, he reached out and grabbed her arm. "Where are you going?"

"I'm going to walk home."

"Walk? It's raining, Ariel."

"I won't melt."

He scowled down at the rain spots on the tips of his polished shoes. "No. But walking in the rain is a good way for me to ruin my suit."

She slid her gaze over his attire, then focused on his hand. As he released her, she reminded him, "I didn't ask you to walk with me."

"I'll drive you." Pete motioned toward his blue Mazda RX-7. "My car is over there. Wait until the rain lets up a little. Then I'll get it."

"I'm going now."

He fumbled in his pants' pocket and produced the car keys. "Stay," he said on an exasperated sigh. "I'll get it now."

"All the way across the street," Ariel taunted him. "Won't your suit get wet?"

His head snapped in her direction. The annoyance in his dark eyes was a warning to her. Ariel took a step back, but he moved his face within inches of hers and whispered between clenched teeth, "I'll get it now."

Stupidly she'd forgotten the fierceness of a temper that rarely stirred. She reared back her head. "Don't be stubborn."

"Who's stubborn?"

"You're stubborn," she managed as he stepped closer, backing her against the wall. Trapped, she was stunned by his nearness in the same way that the sharp, quick prick of a bee sting immobilized the body with momentary pain and panic.

"Now, stay," he said.

She skimmed his expensive suit. It was a nice one, and within it were equally nice shoulders and a well-formed body that enticed a lover's touch.

At the moment she was her own worst enemy, she realized. Battling the direction of her thoughts, she considered instead her own outfit. Her jeans would repel the rain. And her gauzy blouse would dry in minutes, while his suit, even at the hands of an experienced dry-cleaner, would never be the same again.

"You shouldn't be the one to get the car. I should." She snatched the keys dangling from his hand, infuriated that her steady breathing had changed abruptly when he'd moved so close to her. "If you insist, then I'll be the one to get the car."

"You will not."

Ariel slipped beneath his arm and ran out from under the overhang and down the steps. "Stay there. I'll bring it to you," she yelled back.

As she dashed around puddles in the street Pete scrunched his shoulders and darted out into the rain. He could easily have outmatched her strides, but he paced himself to reach the car door at the same moment she did.

Laughing, she looked up at him, which restirred memories, warmed his blood. The wet face so near his ignited the blood that coursed through his veins. She'd stared up at him the same way when they'd taken a shower together. Her eyes had danced, and her playful smile had added a glow of pink to her creamy complexion, and the moisture on her skin had beckoned his lips then, too. "You drive me crazy," he said softly, bending his head toward hers.

She took a step back from him for distance. He moved with her. She didn't want this. It was insane. Just being with him unlocked enough hurt within her; they couldn't be lovers again.

"Ariel, I've missed you."

"Too late."

"Why?"

"It's just too late," she insisted, squirming within the circle of his arms and facing the car to push the key into the lock.

"It's never too late," he murmured against her neck.

Her body went soft against his. Turning around, facing him, responding, was the easy way. She battled to have the will and the strength to choose the more difficult path. She stared down at the key in her hand. "Don't count on what isn't going to happen."

"Because you don't care?" Pete slid his hand up slowly from her waist. Beneath his palm her heart hammered a wild message to him, contradicting everything she'd said.

Her pulse pounded at her temples as he pressed a wispy kiss along the curve of her jaw. She was losing. She moaned softly and laid her forehead against the wet car window.

The total helplessness inherent in the act stunned him. Gently he pressed his mouth against her hair. For a second he inhaled deeply to absorb her scent and lock it in his memory. But he took no more than a second. He knew he was hurting her.

She was a natural fighter, a spirited feminine warrior who'd have proven her mettle against Indians during pioneer days, who'd have resisted all restraints on her freedom, who'd have marched in demonstrations, declaring her views. And he was breaking her strength, snatching it from her.

Lightly he touched her hair, smoothed it, then reached around her to unlock the car.

She scrambled for control as she walked around the car and slid in and across the seat. She felt as if she were sinking into a whirling abyss where escape was impossible. Emotions too strong to resist pulled at her. His touch and the heat of his mouth on her, after so many years when she'd assured herself that she no longer wanted them, bathed her in a shower of confusion.

Pete slid behind the steering wheel and inched his way out of the wet suit jacket. He tossed it in the back seat and tugged at his tie. It followed the jacket. He flicked on the ignition. He flicked on the windshield wipers. Then he switched everything off. Only the quick, rhythmic beat of the rain on the car's roof penetrated the silence between him and Ariel. He shifted on the seat to look at her, aching to touch her. Instead he gripped the steering wheel. "I made a mistake."

She tightened her fingers on the strap of her purse. Quite possibly she'd fooled herself all these years, she thought. She wasn't as strong as she'd always believed she was.

Tentatively he touched her hair. "Is there anyone else, Ariel?"

She knew she should lie. "No," she answered truthfully.

"Don't you get lonely?"

Afraid she'd weaken and move closer to him, she plastered her back against the car door. "Do you?"

"I have been for a long time."

His voice was too soft, too compelling, too convincing. She remained silent for a long moment, afraid to speak, afraid she'd say words that would bring him back into her life.

"Are you?" he asked.

"I'm not going to answer that." She raised her chin a notch. She refused to give him any ammunition. "I read a lot. Maybe you should," she quipped. "Then you wouldn't be so lonely."

Pete draped an arm over the steering wheel and released a mirthless laugh. Tension hung like a thick opaque curtain between them. He was pushing too hard. He knew her well enough to predict how she'd respond if he kept doing that. She'd resist. *Back off*, he warned himself as he saw too much confusion, too much hurt, in her frown. "What books do you read?"

A second passed before she realized he'd shifted moods on her. She felt the tension easing away. He was allowing it to disappear and she briefly wished that he wouldn't. If such sensitivity no longer existed, then resisting him would be easier. She felt a tug at her heart. "All kinds," she answered, a little muddled.

He smiled then, relieved to see her relax. If he wanted her back, he'd better quit steamrolling. He'd never get her that way. Fortunately patience was one of his finer qualities. Pete switched on the ignition again. "Still like salted pretzels with gobs of mustard?"

"Yes."

"I'll drive to—"

"Pete, you're not going to waltz back into my life."

"And afterward we could—"

"No."

"Come on, Ariel. I'm new in town. I don't know nobody, and..."

Laughter rippled from her throat. His dark hair dripping, he looked like a wet puppy. She watched a rivulet of moisture cut across his jaw and down his neck. Unfortunately for her, he was good-looking even when soaking wet. "Robert Redford delivered those lines much better in *The Sting*."

"They worked for him." He inclined his head, questioning, "What about me?"

Ariel released an exasperated sigh. "All right. Two pretzels, then you drop me off at my store."

"I could wait around. You might get hungry again. Or we could go to a movie."

She'd forgotten, she realized, that he'd pursued her the same way before. He'd worn down her resistance, charming her with his resolute personality and gentle manner like an iron hand in a velvet glove. He'd seduced her at all levels, using his intelligence, his thoughtfulness, his passion.

She'd never known a man who'd revealed sensitivity so freely, without feeling that his masculinity was threatened. She'd never laughed so much with anyone before him. Or since. She'd never known the same consuming madness during lovemaking with anyone but him.

He pulled cautiously into traffic. "A movie?"

"Two pretzels," Ariel returned. "I'm not promising more than that."

"It's a start."

Chapter Four

Ariel's resistance proved stronger than she'd expected. Two pretzels. No movie.

Though she regretted the decision and spent the night fighting an urge to wallow in self-pity, she awoke the next morning with a glaring awareness that he'd hurt her before.

She padded on bare feet into the kitchen, recognizing that a battle was beginning. She'd wanted to go to that movie to be with Pete. She longed for the sound of his voice and the sight of his smile, but did any of that matter if it meant risking her heart?

No, she declared, slicing an orange and squeezing it flat. Unconsciously she began humming.

It was a bad sign.

At a tender age she'd seen the movie *The King and I*. After listening to Deborah Kerr singing and whistling her way through uncertainty, Ariel had taken the lyrical message to heart. Always lousy at whistling, she usually hummed when troubled or frightened. If thoughts of Pete stirred such a response, she was definitely in trouble. She wouldn't hum unless she felt uncertain. Of course, she did, she reflected. She was vulnerable to Pete; she was also determined to be no man's doormat. Did he believe that she'd welcome him with waiting arms after he'd left her? Well, she'd show him that she . . .

The thought hung unfinished as the phone rang. Ariel stared at it for a long moment, all her bravado slithering away like a retreating snake. Drawing a long breath, she reached for the receiver, warning herself to be firm if she heard Pete's voice in the next few seconds.

"Ms. Hammond, this is Detective Hernandez."

Her breathing returned to normal. "Yes, Sergeant." Cradling the receiver between her jaw and shoulder, she ground the second half of the orange onto the squeezer. "I'm glad you called. I was getting worried."

"We have a reprieve," he cut in.

"A reprieve?"

"Siske won't be contacting you for a little while."

Ariel stopped squeezing the orange, grasped the receiver, and frowned at it. "He won't?" she responded, puzzled that he had such knowledge.

"No, he won't. He's in jail."

Her shoulders drooped as tension poured out of her. "Then someone else complained about him and you arrested him," she said, feeling relief. Bravery and courage were fleeting emotions. More than once since she'd talked to the sergeant, she'd reconsidered her intent to resist Siske.

"No, I'm sorry to say that you're still our only source to nail him for extortion."

Ariel dumped the juice, including the seeds, into a glass and swallowed a quick mouthful. "Then why is he in jail?"

"Unfortunately not all of the men in the department know what is going on." His token laugh failed to slip some humor into their conversation.

At the moment Ariel doubted she had a funny bone.

When she didn't return a polite laugh, he went on in his usual serious tone. "Sometimes the right hand doesn't know what the left is doing. That sort of thing." At her continued silence he said, "Siske was stopped for speeding and brought in for a breathalyzer test."

"He was drunk?"

"No, he wasn't. But the computer traced an arm-long list of unpaid speeding tickets against him and a failure to appear at a previous court date."

"So he's sitting now and waiting for bail?" She leaned against the wall. "But he'll eventually come to my store again."

"Not for a while. And that's good. It gives us time to plan. I'm supposed to see my superior this afternoon. I should have a definite plan for you soon. In the meantime, don't worry. We're checking to see if there are any other open warrants against him."

" 'Don't worry,' " Ariel parroted worriedly, unable to forget the detective's words that Siske was the extortion ring's muscle man.

"Relax," he soothed. "I have a squad car regularly patroling your area. If Siske shows up, I'll be radioed. We'll protect you."

Ariel muttered polite responses, pretending reassurance, but she was nervous. She was scared.

She set down the receiver and reasoned with herself. Siske hadn't threatened her yet; he'd only talked about damaging her store. But if she stalled too long, he'd probably intensify his pressure. Her imagination took over. In one movie several store owners had been badly beaten for refusing to make such payments.

She gulped down the rest of the orange juice, then wandered into the bedroom.

While dressing, she thought more about that movie. How had the proprietors stopped the man? They'd banded together—under a cinema hero's leadership, of course. Well, the shopkeepers on her street didn't have a Rambo type running around to protect and organize them, but she had to do something, she decided, heading toward the door.

Ariel stared at Seymour Tremble, owner of a small antique shop at the end of the block. His name suited him. He trembled. He shook his fleshy face and wagging jowls and refused her idea of banding together. His wife Lelia, a small, gray-haired woman who barely reached her husband's shoulder, responded for both of them.

"We can't do that. You're young. You're not afraid. You can fight him. But this—" she said, gesturing with her arm in a sweeping motion "—this is all we have. If he wrecks our store, then what do we do?"

Ariel wanted to remind them that they could lose the store if they didn't fight Siske. But staring into two aged, troubled faces stirred a memory of her grandmother. When she'd been alive, she'd had the same panicked look whenever her social security check hadn't arrived on time.

Ariel nodded understandingly and strolled to the next store. Jane Zimmerman sold musical instruments. Her husband had died a year ago, leaving her with three children to raise. Jane managed to stay in business because of the college's extensive music program. As the woman denied that Siske had ever contacted her, which Ariel was certain was a lie, Ariel scanned the displays of violins and cellos. Her gaze settled on the eighteenth-century violin locked inside a glass display case.

Again, Ariel said nothing and trudged to the next door. Emanuel Varquez was a middle-aged man with an overabundant middle. He operated Varquez's Weaving Shop with his son Carlos.

Ariel stood amid the displays of original Chimayo rugs, blankets, pillows, coats and vests. The handiwork was exquisite, the craft having been passed on from generation to generation.

The moment she mentioned Siske, Emanuel's eyes clouded with worry, but he shook his head as if bewildered. He'd lived in the United States too long to pretend that he wasn't comprehending what she was asking. Standing behind the counter, Emanuel's nineteen-year-old son Carlos gave a slow nod, assuring her that Emanuel's response was a phony one.

After several minutes of Ariel's prodding, Emanuel finally admitted "Yes! Yes, he has been here."

"And my father paid him," Carlos informed her.

Emanuel slammed his palm down on the countertop. "In Mexico, children did not speak unless their elders told them to."

Carlos met his father's stare squarely. "This is not Mexico."

"No respect!" Emanuel yelled.

"I respect you, but I know it is wrong for you to pay him any more money."

Ariel knew she had an ally. "Mr. Varquez, if we pay Siske, he'll keep asking for more and more money. We have to stop him."

"I told him this," Carlos said.

Emanuel swung his bulky frame around and faced his son, wagging a finger at him. "We must not anger him. This business is for you. As it was my father's and now mine, someday it will be yours. You do not want it?"

"Every day I work here with you. We work side by side to keep our business. But Ariel, she is right. We will lose the shop. This man will keep coming back for more and more money. And then we will have no more to give him."

Ariel grabbed the opportunity to elicit help. "I thought if we had a meeting, we could discuss the problem. I've gone to the police and . . ."

Emanuel shook his head wildly. "No! No, meeting. You will have more trouble." He sliced a meaty hand through the air. "We will not come," he said angrily, and whirled away, heading toward a back stockroom.

Carlos sent her a sympathetic look. "He is frightened."

"Who isn't?"

"Some less than others, I would say." He smiled at Ariel. "I will come to this meeting. I will be there."

Ariel breathed deeply. "You'll come? Oh, Carlos, thank you. Would you try to talk to the Trembles? And Jane Zimmerman. See if you can persuade them."

"I will try. I will talk to my father, too," he said in the tolerant tone of a son with a stubborn father. "But to talk to him is not easy."

Ariel smiled. "Just try. That's all I ask."

"And if no one else comes?"

Her stomach rolled. "Then I'm on my own."

Pete aimed a paper airplane at the wastebasket beside his desk and gingerly tossed it in. For a long moment his gaze shifted from the rubber tree plant in a corner of his office to a copy of a van Gogh on a nearby wall. He stared at the yellow and orange and red mass and thought of Ariel's hair. When sunlight danced across it, streaks of gold mingled with the red.

With a mumbled curse, Pete swiveled the chair and fixed his gaze on the glossy portfolio he'd been studying.

All morning his concentration had wavered as he'd wondered what Ariel's problem was. Why didn't she tell him? Why did she think she had to handle it on her own? His own thought made him smile. Ariel believed in standing alone. People come into the world alone, she'd said, and people leave that way. Leaning on someone else wasn't her way. Her independence drove him mad sometimes. Like now, he mused, feeling more than a cursory curiosity about what was going on in her life.

She'd tell him to mind his own business, he reminded himself. And she'd have every right to say that.

"You'd better snap out of it." Muriel Ellerway's scratchy voice intruded on his thoughts. She'd been Pete's secretary in New York. She was a prim, proper-looking woman in her early fifties who always wore gray suits and high-necked blouses with a brooch pinned at the neck. She appeared perfect for a secretary of a Bryant and Bryant consultant. Pete considered her indispensable and had cajoled her into making the move with him. For weeks she'd resisted. Then he'd made the magic announcement. Before the end of the year, construction would begin on a dog-racing track in Albuquerque. Muriel loved to gamble.

"That reporter is here. If you don't get your act together, two to one she'll be writing that Bryant and

Bryant associates daydream ways to handle their clients' business.''

Pete pushed back his chair. "What does she look like?"

"Medium."

He laughed. "Medium what?"

"Everything. Medium height, medium-colored brown hair, medium looks." Muriel rocked her hand. "Closer to blah than pretty."

"Okay, send her in," he said, standing and slipping on his suit jacket.

Muriel stopped at the door. "She also looks hungry."

"Hungry for what?"

"A nice, meaty story," she said slowly, stressing the words.

Pete released a long breath. Just what he wanted. Besides trying to get a foothold in the Southwest for Bryant and Bryant, he'd also have to pass the inspection of some reporter from *Business Scope*, one of the most influential business magazines in the United States, whose reporters showed no compunction about revealing any skeletons in corporate closets.

Pete yanked at the bottom of his vest while firmly cussing the public relations people at the home office for approving these arrangements. He didn't need some news hound standing over his shoulder, rating him for J.C. Bryant and the world.

Pete rounded his desk to meet her halfway. She's not here to do a hatchet job, he reminded himself. At least that's what the PR people in New York had told him. He hoped they were telling the truth.

He readjusted his tie and watched the doorknob turn. As the door flung open he concentrated on the slim, long face of the woman standing before him. Carol Jamison smiled, seemed pleasant and, Pete noted with a glance at her tape recorder, eager.

He ushered her into the room. As she passed him, he smelled her perfume, something strong and lingering. His mind betrayed him and for a brief second his thoughts strayed to the light, flowery scent of Ariel's. Annoyed with himself, he stepped around his desk, cautioning himself that thinking about Ariel at a moment like this might lead to professional disaster.

Ariel visited four more shopkeepers. Three refused to talk about anything but the street repairs last month, the rain yesterday, and the escalation of taxes. One shopkeeper, Judd Calhoun, an artist who displayed his work in his store, spoke openly and freely to her.

"You and your mother must be the last two on the block to be contacted by him."

"When did Siske contact you?"

"Several days ago."

"And what did you say?"

"I was angry enough to strangle him."

Success at that might be possible for him, Ariel thought. Calhoun wasn't a tall man, but he was broad. If nothing else, he could use the numerous turquoise rings on his fingers as brass knuckles. "Did you go to the police?"

He stepped around the desk at the back of his gallery and reached down. "I noticed your window was broken."

"Siske did that."

Calhoun stood with a canvas in his hands and turned it to face Ariel. A large rip ran diagonally across the center of the painting, breaking the serenity of a brilliant mango and fuchsia sunset.

Ariel shivered.

"I don't know who ruined the painting, but the next day Siske came in. He strolled around the gallery, then stopped beside my desk and stared at the painting. 'Think about protection,' he said." Calhoun set the painting on his desk. "No, I didn't go to the police. And if he finds out that you did, you might end up with more than a broken window."

Ariel didn't know what else to say. Calhoun had already felt Siske's devastating tactics.

As she started for the door, Calhoun called out her name.

Ariel paused and looked back.

"I'll be at your meeting."

Ariel walked back to her store. Two people had said yes, but she needed more. Through the morning she worried about talking to her mother. It was wrong not to tell her, but Ariel was never sure how her mother would react.

At noon Rosie arrived at the store. Ariel still hadn't made a decision about her mother, but she'd decided to handle problems one at a time. Pete first. With an idea taking hold, she hurried next door to the flower shop.

Pete reviewed the portfolio of a new client. He heard the click of the office door but didn't look up at Muriel. The executive was losing money because he'd invested only in tax-exempt securities.

"These were just delivered," his secretary said.

"Set them on my desk, Muriel." Pete continued to stare at the information before him. The man needed investments that would force him to pay some taxes but offer him greater potential for capital appreciation.

"But they'll wilt."

"Papers don't..." Looking up, Pete frowned. "Don't say a word," he ordered as he stared at the bouquet of yellow daffodils in her hand.

"I thought there was a mistake, but the delivery boy double-checked his sheet and announced that these were for Pete Turner."

"There's no mistake." Pete half stood and bent forward toward her to peer at the flowers. "No card?"

Muriel's hand whipped out from behind her back. "Sure is. Your new lady friend has panache."

Pete sat down again. "Did you steam the card open?"

"Would I do that?"

Pete sent her a skeptical look.

"It's one of those thick white envelopes," Muriel grumbled, handing it to him. "The kind that you can't see through even when you hold it up to a light."

Pete slipped the letter opener under the envelope flap. "You have an unscrupulous streak."

Her pleased cackle drifted back to him before she closed the door. Incredibly his heart jumped as he read the card's message: "One o'clock. In the park."

Pete glanced at his watch and shoved back his chair. The allure had returned. Who was he kidding? It had never left.

As he walked from his office he conjured up an image of Ariel, her blue eyes laughing, her flaming red hair flying beneath the wind's caress. No other woman had ever made him ache for the sound of her voice or the gentleness of her touch. No other woman had ever sparked something wild within him that made him want to throw caution to the wind.

Chapter Five

Some people arrived late often. Ariel was one of them. She always thought she had enough time. Yet inevitably she would be sidetracked by something.

Jogging across the grass toward the southern section of the park, she knew that Pete would be waiting, and if she offered an excuse, he'd nod and smile and understand. And damn it, she didn't want him to do any of that. If he would be angry with her for being late, she could start a list of reasons why she didn't want him back into her life.

Her world hadn't stopped when he'd left. And she hadn't yearned for Pete Turner's return, she reminded herself firmly.

Sounds from a nearby zoo drifted through the air. Ariel skimmed the couples picnicking on blankets until she found one dark-haired man alone. Sitting under a tree, he gazed at the distant mountain peaks. While he looked relaxed, as if he didn't have a care in the world, she was charged with nervous energy. Aware she'd quickened her stride, she immediately slowed it to a saunter, refusing to appear overeager to be with him.

Sprawled on a blanket, Pete leaned back against a tree and enjoyed her approach. He'd missed the sight of her easy, loose stride, the swing of her arm, the slight sway of her hips. Sunlight poured down, bathing her sun-brushed skin and her yellow jumpsuit with a warm glow. He watched and he ached for what had once been between them, for what still lingered in his heart.

When she plopped down beside him, setting a small picnic basket between them, the scent of her flowery fragrance pummeled his senses. Years ago he would have reached for her, kissed her, and she'd have laughed. Now he could only torment himself with memories.

Ariel flipped open the basket. "So you came."

"Did you really think that I wouldn't?" he answered lazily.

She dug into the basket and avoided his eyes. "Don't you have a daily calendar somewhere with something to do every hour?"

"I try to avoid business lunches." He reached for one of the cans of soda.

His fingertips grazed her knuckles during the exchange. The contact was brief, but not brief enough for Ariel. Her heart jumped and muscles tensed, warning her that the battle had begun again.

"Thank you for the flowers." He inclined his head to see her face. Curls framed her cheeks as she dug again into the basket. "Why did you send them?"

"On a whim."

"You could have called and asked for a date."

"It's not a date," she returned quickly. "And calling is too—too..."

"Too ordinary."

"Is it a first for you?" she asked, making much about setting out napkins.

He touched her chin and forced her to look at him. "Yes."

Run her mind screamed. *Get away now.* But she knew she couldn't. If she did, she'd reveal too much to him. "Good," she returned brightly, struggling not to remember the nights when his strong but gentle touch had lingered on her body. She had to be as firm as the granite cliff in the distance. "Since I made the date..."

"So this is a date?"

"A lunch," she insisted, setting a wrapped sandwich before him. "This is a business lunch."

Pete cocked a brow. "Business?" Cautiously he unwrapped the sandwich, then grimaced at the peanut butter and jelly oozing from the sides of the bread. "What business do we have to discuss?"

"Us. I've..." She cut her words short as he whipped a picnic basket out from behind the tree. "I decided to meet you because you were pushing our relationship."

"Pushing?" Pete sent her an enigmatic smile, then concentrated on opening a bottle of wine.

"I don't want to repeat a mistake I made before," she said, her curiosity piqued by his basket.

Pete offered her a glass of wine. "We weren't a mistake."

"I meant when I married Jonathan."

Pete nodded, setting a cheese board on the blanket. The sharp, distinct aroma of Brie mingled with the sweet fragrance of Chablis. "I agree."

Ariel ignored his quick comment. "He wanted an orderly life. He wanted everything in the proper slot. Meals at specific times, his shirts hung a certain way on color-coded hangers."

"I don't have those."

She almost smiled. "And his dresser drawers were labeled as if in some fit of amnesia he'd forget that the socks belonged in the far right corner. He organized everything. From the spices in my kitchen, which he arranged alphabetically, to the bottles in the medicine cabinet, which he lined up according to size."

Pete regarded her over the rim of his glass. "I never did that."

"No, you never did," she admitted. "You allowed me my clutter, but—"

"Back off a moment. I am not that much of a stickler for order," he said defensively, tearing a portion of bread from the long, crusty loaf, "and you damn well know it."

Ariel raised a brow skeptically.

"I tore the Sunday paper apart."

"Then neatly restacked it."

"Because you liked to tear it apart yourself. And I left the cap off toothpaste tubes. Don't you remember that?"

"I remember." Magical moments flashed into her mind. They softened her. They annoyed her. "So you bought the new pump style," she reminded him.

"I hated taking out the garbage," he countered.

"So I did that, and you washed pots and pans because you liked to polish the copper bottoms."

"I didn't like to do it."

Ariel gave him a knowing smile.

"Okay, I liked doing it," Pete admitted grudgingly. "But after sitting for hours in an office, moving nothing more than a pencil, I enjoyed using elbow grease on something. But if we were so different, then why did it work for us?"

Ariel frowned, slightly dumbfounded by the logic in his question. Looking away, she realized he'd spotted the weakness in her plan. She'd meant to explain what marriage had been like for her with Jonathan. Pete could relate to someone like him. And yet for two years she and Pete had lived together in perfect harmony.

"There's nothing wrong with planning," he said.

"He didn't mean planning like you do," she admitted. "Sometimes you'd say, 'In a couple of years let's do this or that.' He'd say, 'In one year and three months we'll buy a house.' He had everything scheduled. Marriage at twenty-eight, a home at thirty. One dog, two children."

"Did you want children?"

Ariel nodded. "But he wasn't into parenthood at that point. He decided everything in life should come at the appropriate time. When we moved to California, he was in a building-his-career stage."

Pete stared at the liquid in his glass. Her comment pricked his conscience, extracting and forcing him to face truth along with regret. His own goals had paralleled Wessell's.

"He was possessed with his success and the name he was making for himself. He had the star syndrome."

"A banker?"

Ariel matched his wry smile. "A banker. He had that 'I'm wonderful' complex. He made me feel as if I was supposed to be honored that he'd chosen me for his wife." Ariel shifted and sat back on her heels. "I didn't take orders very well. I wanted to do things that he didn't like."

"Like what?"

"The store. During the time I was growing up, my father talked of traveling. In my way, opening an import store makes me feel close to him. The store is something I really wanted, but Jonathan thought it wouldn't look right for his wife to be a salesclerk."

Pete gave a shake of his head. "That doesn't make sense. If you own the store, you're the proprietor."

"He couldn't see the difference. It was one of many things that eventually made us just a statistic."

"Why did you marry him? And don't say rebound. Something else made you marry him."

Ariel sipped the wine. "He wanted what I wanted."

"Wessell?" Puzzled, Pete frowned, unable to think of one thing Wessell had in common with Ariel. His favorite topic of conversation had always focused on the economy. "What? What did he want that you wanted?" Pete asked, struggling to remember Wessell's past conversations. "Did you think he wanted to travel because he gave dissertations at football games about Malaysia being a developing nation and having a diverse export base?"

At his recollection, amusement sprang into her eyes. "He did do that, didn't he?"

"Yes, he did. So what did he want that you wanted?"

Ariel met his gaze squarely, wondering if he was prepared for her answer. "To get married."

He felt as if he'd been punched in the stomach. A frown lined his forehead.

"Don't do that," Ariel urged, running a fingertip along the crease between his brows as if by touch she could erase the line. "Four years have passed, Pete. We can't do anything about that time anymore. You and I didn't make it before. And I didn't make it with Jonathan. And that's my point. I'm not going to repeat my mistake."

"What you're saying makes no sense."

"Yes, it does."

"Not to me," he countered. Watching her lips tighten into a stubborn, straight line, he saw the futility in continuing the argument. He drained the wine in his glass before asking, "I thought you'd travel. Why didn't you?"

"I wanted to travel with someone. It wouldn't have mattered unless I could share all the new sights with someone." The thoughtful look in his eyes made her want to touch his hand. He was considering her words, weighing them. Did he feel as much pain when he heard them as she had felt while saying them? Drawing a long breath, she reached for the loaf of bread. "Did you like New York?"

Pete grabbed the loaf first, needing something physical to keep from reaching out and pulling her into his arms. "It breathes," he answered, breaking a hunk from the loaf and handing it to her. "The city has personality."

"Fanciful talk, for you."

"Occasionally I was fanciful, wasn't I?" he asked, and grazed a finger across the top of her hand.

Another tug at her heart. Another weakened moment. How many was she strong enough to resist? she wondered. "Pete, don't. I've tried to explain. Did you expect to return and find everything the same as before?"

"We didn't part angry."

She looked past him, watching children racing from the swings to the playground slide. "No, we didn't, but—"

"We parted as friends."

"We are, but—"

He slipped his hand over hers. "A lot of buts."

Unwittingly her gaze returned to meet his. "I don't want to start this up again."

"You don't want to? Or you think you don't?" he asked, sliding his fingers around her wrist and feeling the steady beat of her pulse quicken.

"If I did, then I'd be fanciful."

He tipped his head questioningly.

"I know better now."

"About me?"

"About you and me. We wouldn't make it."

"We did."

"I mean forever," Ariel explained, despite her hidden desire to let him win this disagreement.

"Because you and Wessell didn't?"

"That's right."

"I'm not Wessell."

Pain begot pain. "You're close," she whispered.

He winced.

"I'm sorry." She hadn't meant to hurt him. All she wanted to do was protect herself. "Pete, you're not exactly like him, but you care about presenting a certain image. You follow the same life plan. You never act impulsively or rashly. Every single thing you do is well thought out before you act."

He smiled wryly then, the gleam in his eyes purely masculine. "Not everything."

Don't grin like that at me, she thought. *Don't make me remember other times when you've looked that way.* "Don't be cute. I'm talking about decisions," she quipped, struggling to resist a yearning to try again with him, to believe that this time would be different. "Some things you have no control over."

"Yes, I do."

She chomped on a wedge of cheese. "You know what I mean, and you're deliberately being difficult."

"I'm here, aren't I?"

Ariel stopped chewing and stared questioningly at him.

"Impulse. Pure impulse brought me here."

Ariel's gaze slid to the lunch basket beside her. "And with you, you brought a well-planned lunch basket."

"Be grateful. We could have been stuck with peanut butter and jelly sandwiches."

"I like peanut butter and jelly sandwiches."

"You like Chablis, too. And Brie. And crusty French bread from the Café Français."

"Technically, what you're doing is cheating."

He heard a hint of amusement in her voice. Anger was the most difficult emotion for her to maintain. Even during some of their fiercest arguments, something would tickle her funny bone and spring a smile to her face. As the corners of her lips twitched, he sensed a tug-of-war taking place within her.

"You know my favorites and use them to your advantage," she said.

"And I plan to keep doing that."

Exasperated, she sighed heavily before looking up from the bread in her hand.

He grinned and waited. For an unpredictable woman, she reacted predictably. A smile crept slowly up her face.

"Is this a whim?" she asked.

"I never do anything on a whim, Ariel. You've spent the last fifteen minutes telling me that." He refilled his glass and clinked it against hers in a toast. "Haven't you?"

She stared into his eyes. Their darkness produced a familiar sensation inside her, the same warmth she'd felt when she'd first fallen in love with him. "You didn't plan well this time."

He heard a tease in her voice. "Why didn't I?"

"You always brought the newspaper crossword puzzle along on picnics."

Pete whipped the newspaper from the basket. "Anything to please you," he said softly, setting it and a pencil on the blanket before her.

Picking up the paper and pencil, Ariel considered the last few moments. Her plan to set him straight had gone astray. Maybe she needed a new plan.

No strategy would work, she realized. She wanted to forget about planning and just let her emotions guide her, but the foolishness of such action would haunt her. If they'd been wrong for each other before, then what had changed? Nothing.

As a cuckoo at the back of the store signaled five o'clock, she yanked her shoulder bag from the floor behind the counter. All day she'd tried to accomplish something, but every time she'd plunge one step forward she'd skid two steps back. Crates remained unopened; her mother hadn't been told about Siske; and Pete had inched his way further into her life again.

Determined to make some kind of progress, she announced, "I'm going to leave now."

Perched on a stool, a polishing rag in her hand, Rosie looked up from the silver candle holder in her hand.

"Business has been slow, so if you want to catch up on your reading or sewing, go ahead," Ariel told her.

Rosie joined her behind the counter and set her oversized carry-all bag on it.

"How far are you to reaching your goal?" Ariel asked.

"I've read *Crime and Punishment* and *The Scarlet Letter*."

Ariel touched her shoulder. "All the classics first?"

"I thought if I began reading them this summer, then it would put me ahead of the required reading for my fall course." Rosie grinned then, her round face filling out and puffing her cheeks so they resembled a chipmunk's. "But I give myself a break in between." She reached into her bag and pulled out a romance novel. "Have to keep the fires ignited."

Ariel laughed. "Is there a new man in your life?"

"Don't I wish. How about you? Have you seen the yellow daffodils man yet?"

"I've seen him."

"So?"

"So you keep *your* fires ignited."

Rosie clucked her tongue. "No fire, huh?"

Too much, Ariel thought. *Far too much.*

Pete slouched on the chair in his father's living room and nursed a beer. During the afternoon Carol Jamison had returned to his office and glued herself to his side while she gathered more information about the services that Bryant and Bryant offered. Pete felt that he'd sailed through the interview. Only at one moment had perspiration dotted the back of his neck.

As Evan joined him in the living room, Pete relived the moment for him. "Carol Jamison latched on to the idea of emphasizing company loyalty. She zeroed in on Muriel, deciding to include her in the article. It was my own fault. Stupidly I mentioned that Muriel had left New York and moved to New Mexico to help me establish the new office."

"You always gave me the impression that you considered her an excellent secretary." Evan picked up the television remote-control unit and flicked off a local news program.

"The best, really. But the love of her life is a sure bet at the racetrack."

"Since you're smiling, I'd guess everything went well."

"Fortunately she hid her racing forms." Pete's grin slipped. "But Jamison makes me jumpy."

"You have a good record with Bryant and Bryant."

"I'm not sure anyone is ever done being scrutinized by J.C. Bryant."

Evan peered over his glasses at his son. "Why not find another company?"

"Because it's one of the most respected in the country. It's the one I want to work for." Pete shifted on the chair and leaned forward. "Listen, are you free tonight?"

"Most days and nights. In another month that question will require a different response. As soon as classes start, my life of leisure ends. What did you have in mind?"

"A ball game. You still have season passes, don't you?"

Evan nodded and glanced at the grandfather clock in the hallway.

"You had other plans?"

"Ginnie," Evan said simply.

Pete held out his hands in a casual gesture. "Then some other time."

"She loves baseball games."

Pete eased out of the chair. "No, I don't want to get in the way." He stood in the middle of the living room, glancing around at its shelves of his father's books.

Though the surroundings were the familiar ones he'd known while growing up, something was different. Music, he realized. Seconds ago his father had flicked on the stereo. Pete cocked his head and listened. Instead of Bach, the rinky-dink tones of a ragtime song filled the air. "Dad?"

Evan paused in midstride on his way to the telephone.

"I don't want to interfere," Pete said. "I just—I know you can get lonely. Maybe you have been and I've been too busy to notice. But don't do anything...anything rash."

"Don't be silly. I've never been an impulsive person."

"You've also never been interested in someone like Virginia before, either."

Evan's arm circled Peter's shoulder. "Do you know your biggest problem?"

"I'm sure you're going to tell me."

"You're too serious, Pete. You were like that when you were young, too. You thought about world problems." Evan squeezed his son's shoulder. "Even at the age of ten."

Pete laughed.

"Now," Evan insisted, "I'll call Ginnie, and then we'll all go to the ball game."

"Dad, I—"

"But first we'll eat. I'm starving. Chinese," he stated. "I have a craving for chicken chow mein."

Ariel wandered along the back row of plush seats in the college theater. A small, private institution, it stressed art and theater. The community nurtured and supported all the cultural events, including charity and summer-stock theater performances. Amateur thespians enjoyed the limelight for several months every summer. Virginia Hammond was one of them.

Ariel strolled down the aisle past rows of seats. From the stage, voices rose.

As quietly as possible she pushed down a seat at the end of the row and listened to her mother delivering Bianca's speech that books and music would keep her company until her ill-tempered sister Kate married. Then Bianca could find her own love.

Victims of last-minute nerves, someone flubbed a line, two of the stagehands briefly squabbled about the position of a prop, and one of the performers tripped over a misplaced potted plant.

At the announcement that rehearsal was over Virginia glided from the stage. Seeing Ariel, she waved, then bustled down the stairs to the theater aisle.

"Sweetheart, how nice that you came. Have you been here long?"

"I arrived a few minutes ago. The play is sounding very good."

Virginia hooked her arm with Ariel's and conspiratorially leaned her head close. "Some of the performers are jittery. In two weeks' time they'll have calmed down. But Baptista has an atrocious memory. I know we're all going to be whispering cues to him all night. And Hortensio needs mouthwash."

Ariel smiled as they proceeded up the aisle. "Have you told him?"

"Oh, no, I couldn't hurt his feelings so. But I pretended my throat was dry and I pulled out a roll of breath mints. Nonchalantly, I suggested he might want one, too."

Though Ariel started to return her smile, Virginia's faded suddenly.

"Why did you let me ramble so? You must be here for a reason."

"Yes, I—"

"Have you seen Peter?" Virginia asked.

"Yes, I've seen him."

"Oh, dear, then something is wrong."

"No," Ariel protested. "I came to see you and to find out how the play was doing."

Virginia frowned. "Peter hasn't changed, has he?"

Ariel quickened her stride to match her mother's high-energy pace. "He's still gung-ho about work."

"I meant his objection to Evan seeing me."

Ariel weighed her answer carefully, not wanting to bring sadness to her mother. "He's always been cautious."

"Yes, and that is understandable."

"I'm glad you're so understanding."

"You should be, dear. At a tender age Pete coped with something very difficult."

Ariel dug a hand into her purse and rummaged around for sunglasses. "I know his parents' divorce was hard on him."

Virginia slowed her steps. "There was a great deal more to it than that. Didn't he ever talk to you about it?"

"Briefly."

"Only briefly." Her look was disapproving. "Communication is vital in a relationship," Virgina advised. "If you had talked more, then—"

"He never wanted to discuss it."

"I understand," Virginia assured her.

"You keep saying that you understand. Understand what?"

"You can't make someone talk if he doesn't want to, but Peter's concern now for his father makes sense to me."

"Well, it doesn't to me. Pete should be pleased that you're interested in his father. Any man would be lucky to be with you."

Virginia beamed. "There isn't a prejudiced bone in your body, is there?"

Ariel laughed. "Any intelligent person would see how wonderful you are."

"Pete considers many things," Virginia said in an unnaturally serious tone.

"Too many."

"Don't be hard on him. The divorce was difficult enough on him. The scandal must have been agonizing."

Ariel shrugged. "A scandal over what? A man's wife leaving him? That's ridiculous. This isn't the eighteenth century."

Virginia stopped. "You really don't know the whole story, do you?"

Ariel inclined her head questioningly. "What whole story?"

"Peter's mother left with a man quite a bit younger than her. Both of them also were associated with the same college where Evan was a professor. Several days after she took off with him, they had a car accident. The newspapers covered it but also exposed why she and this man were together. The college didn't appreciate one of their professors being linked with that kind of publicity."

"So they requested that he leave?"

"Not at first. Evan told me that he wasn't prepared for her leaving. If he wasn't, it's unlikely their seven-year-old son was, and Evan blames himself for what happened in his career. He said that he acted foolishly. Like a mad-man, he left to track her down. His words, not mine. I can't imagine Evan ignoring his responsibility to the school or his students. But he did."

"What did he do?"

"He tried to convince her to return. Peter was staying with another teacher and his wife during that time." Virginia's voice was filled with compassion. "When Evan returned, the college requested his resignation. Of course, they had a perfectly legitimate reason for doing that. But for the next few years, Evan admitted that life was diffi-cult for Peter and him."

"But he's been on the Sandia Crest College staff for years."

"Yes. Since Peter was thirteen. But there were many hard years in between. So you understand now."

"No, I really don't."

"Peter is worried that I'll do something as impulsive as his mother had and harm Evan. Ariel," Virginia said appealingly, "think. Would you ever have expected Evan to react so impulsively?"

"No, I really wouldn't have."

"Of course not. He and Peter are very cautious, sen-sible men." Her thin brows knitted. "Evan spoke to Pe-ter many times and tried to explain that his own rash actions resulted in his losing that position at the Massa-chusetts college. However, Peter believed his mother's actions pushed his father to act so unnaturally." Her lips curved in a weak smile. "Evan is a dear man. An emo-tional one. And now that his career is stable again, Peter worries about history repeating itself."

Where was the silly woman who couldn't balance her checkbook? Ariel wondered. Her mother's depth of un-derstanding stretched beyond the norm.

"Peter is a strong, loving man. He cares deeply about his father. From past experience, Peter's learned that impulsive actions can lead to disaster."

"Not always."

"No, not always." Virginia brushed a hand across her cheek. "But you and I follow the moment. That's our way. Not theirs," she said, then sniffed suddenly. Without forewarning she shifted the topic of conversation. "I'm absolutely starving. Are you?"

Ariel followed her new mood. "That was the real reason why I came to see you. Are you free for dinner?" she asked, wondering if she could work up the courage to talk to her mother about Siske by the time they were through eating.

"I'd love to, dear. But I have to make one phone call first."

"To Evan?"

"Why, yes."

"Did you have something planned with him this evening?"

Virginia waved a hand at her. "Never mind that." She sniffed hard at the air as if cooking aromas dominated. "Moo goo gai pan," she announced. "I can almost taste it."

Chapter Six

Virginia whipped her canary-yellow Mustang around a corner. "Him's makes wonderful moo goo gai pan."

Ariel nodded, distracted by the heart-shaped balloon attached to the car antenna. "Where did you get the balloon?"

"Evan, of course."

The balloon danced and flipped around to offer Ariel a view of the words printed on the front of it: Evan loves you.

"You'll love the atmosphere," Virginia assured her.

As her mother zipped the car into an unpaved parking area behind the restaurant, Ariel questioned, "Atmosphere?"

It was a bleak-looking adobe building. Despite its plain exterior, cars jammed the parking lot. "When did they open this?"

"A month ago. Maybe two." Virginia switched off the ignition and looked at her daughter. "You've never been here?"

"I didn't even know it existed."

Removing her sunglasses, Ariel preceded Virginia into the restaurant, which wouldn't win an award for its decor. It was a large, square room filled with low tables, colorful pillows, and people. Brightly colored umbrellas hung from the ceiling, and a giant green papier-mâché dragon stood from floor to ceiling in the center of the room. Someone else might have questioned her mother's notion of atmosphere. Ariel no longer did. The restaurant's oddity enticed the patrons, and the loud buzz of voices in conversation was sufficient atmosphere for a woman who truly enjoyed the company of other people.

"Isn't it wonderful?" Virginia said.

Ariel met her mother's bright face. "Wonderful. And crowded. I doubt we'll get a table."

"Oh, we'll get one."

Such optimism surely would be rewarded, Ariel mused.

"Come on, dear."

"Where?" Ariel asked the question to her mother's back.

Virginia wound a swift path around tables as if their destination promised a pot of gold. A treasure of sorts did exist, Ariel realized as she caught a glimpse of Evan's wide grin.

Pete shifted uncomfortably on the pillow, damning his long legs and trying to tuck them into the contortionist's position that resembled the one Evan had taken. The only male in the restaurant who was wearing a suit, he contemplated ways to shed his tie and jacket and roll up the sleeves of his shirt without being too conspicuous.

Preoccupied, his father had his gaze riveted on Virginia approaching their table.

Pete reached up to yank at his tie. His fingers froze as Ariel suddenly plopped down on the pillow beside him. Suspiciously she narrowed her eyes at him, then scowled. Pete couldn't help himself; he smiled.

"Do you wear a suit everywhere now?" Ariel asked while maneuvering a slice of beef between her chopsticks.

"Everywhere," he answered, aware she was annoyed at unwittingly having dinner with him. Her baiting tone didn't faze him. Being with her seemed reward enough.

"Not everywhere?"

He gave her a smirking grin. "I learned that suits and water don't go well together. So I take it off before going in the shower."

"How intelligent of you."

Evan inclined his head. "What in the world are you two talking about?"

"A walk in the rain, Dad," Pete replied.

Virginia passed the soy sauce to her daughter. "Ariel loves to walk in the rain."

Pete's gaze never left Ariel's. "Yes, I know," he said softly. "We met that way."

"You did?" Virginia's voice rose in curiosity. "I never knew how you met. Tell me," she said, propping an elbow on the table and resting her jaw on her palm.

Ariel knew the interested look well. "Nothing overly romantic, Mother."

Pete frowned. "I thought it was."

"You did?"

"Yes, I did. We had a lot of good times when it was raining."

"Like sunshine in the rain," Virginia piped up. "Isn't that poetic. And romantic."

Ariel sent her mother a sharp look. "Evan, are you looking forward to the new semester starting soon?"

"It could be different for me this year."

Virginia leaned close to him, lovingly hooking one arm in his. "He's going to be the head of the history department."

Ariel smiled at her mother's prideful tone. "That's impressive."

"Your mother is forgetting that I have competition."

"You deserve the appointment, Dad."

Virginia held up her hand with crossed fingers. "After he gets it," she said with certainty, "we'll have a celebration dinner."

Ariel returned her mother's smile and nodded, but she noted Pete's frown. He stared down at his plate, his brows knitted in a worried slant that she was familiar with.

The meal passed with relative ease, more than Ariel had anticipated when she'd seen Pete sitting at the table. Virginia rambled on about the play, sharing humorous anecdotes. Laughter circled their table, and if Ariel took the time for an honest second, she had to admit that the evening was a pleasant one. Sipping tea, she watched as her mother distributed a fortune cookie to each of them.

"I think this is the best part of the meal," she said brightly. "Have you noticed that fortune cookies are always optimistic? It's such a wonderful custom." She looked at Evan. "I think I'll buy a bag of them so we can have one after every meal."

Pete shook his head. "They don't really mean anything."

Virginia's smile faded. "Oh, Peter, but they do if you believe they do."

"They're like—" He stopped suddenly, stunned by the sharp jab of a knee against his under the table.

Ariel drilled a look at him, determined to prevent his serious and often cynical attitude from marring her mother's bright evening.

"Did you do that?" he asked.

"Do what?" Ariel asked innocently.

Too innocently. Pete grinned. "Never mind."

Evan frowned. "You two talk in a strange way to each other. It's very difficult to follow your conversations. In fact, they make very little sense."

"Yes, I've noticed that," Virginia said.

Ariel giggled. If anyone's conversation strayed from the norm, it was her mother's. "I guess that was our problem. Peter and I never learned to communicate."

He bent to the side and rubbed at his knee. "I'd say we communicate clearly to each other."

Ariel's eyes danced. "At times I suppose that we did."

"Let's read these now," Virginia said, cracking the cookie.

Evan leaned close to read over her shoulder. "What does yours say?"

Virginia smiled widely. "'There is no instinct like that of the heart,'" she said, and brushed her lips lightly across his cheek.

Ariel watched for a second, then stared down at the cookie in her hands. Her mother's warmth and love for Pete's father was undeniable. It spread, radiating a glow of happiness to anyone near them.

"And yours?" Virginia insisted.

Evan chuckled softly before reading out loud, "'A special time is near.'"

Virginia oohed. "What do you think that means?"

"I know what I hope it means," Evan said.

She laughed with him, then swiveled her head toward Pete. "Open yours, Peter."

Pete stared at the irregular-shaped cookie before him. He classed fortune cookies with Ouija boards and crystal balls. Looking up, he saw his father's expectant grin. Pete picked up the cookie. If his father, the most logical man he knew, could go along with the idea, then he could, Pete decided. He cracked the cookie shell and unfolded the slip of paper. The message was discomforting, hitting him in the gut.

"What does it say?" Evan prodded.

At Pete's pained expression, Ariel looked over his arm to see the words.

"'When you make a mistake, don't look back at it. Correct it,'" she read aloud, then lifted her brows.

"It's a wise message," Evan commented.

Pete gave Ariel a thoughtful smile. "Yes, it is. But it's one I'd already thought about."

"See there," Virginia interjected. "The messages really do tell the future."

Virginia gestured with her head. "It's your turn, Ariel."

Ariel shifted the cookie in her hand, reminding herself that someone ran off hundreds of the little slips of paper. In Chinese restaurants all over the United States, other women were cracking open fortune cookies and reading the same message. A mushy, sentimental message, no doubt. A message she'd rather read while alone.

She grabbed at any distraction. Hearing the sound of voices at the restaurant's entrance, she swiveled a glance over her shoulder. "It's crowding up even more, if that's possible," she said, wondering if an emergency arose how quickly they'd exit from their close—too close—quarters. "Don't you think we should leave?" she suggested, dropping the unopened fortune cookie into her purse.

"I suppose we should," Virginia agreed.

Suddenly restless, Ariel stood first, not waiting for a further response.

She stepped outside ahead of the others. A warm breeze drifted across her face and rustled leaves on a nearby tree. One leaf fluttered on an aimless path across the sidewalk before her. The wind controlled its destiny, but she determined her own, not some whimsical saying stuffed inside a Chinese cookie. Briefly she glanced at the fortune cookie in her purse. Inquisitiveness was sometimes a difficult trait to live with, she mused. She fingered the cookie, then discarded the idea of opening it, her attention shifting to her mother.

One step behind her, Evan stopped and waited until Pete joined them. Linking Virginia's arm with his, Evan announced, "I'll drive to the stadium with Virginia, since she has her car. Pete, you bring Ariel in yours," he called out, already walking away from them.

Ariel stared, dumbfounded, after her mother and Evan. "What—what is he talking about?" she asked, turning to Pete for an answer.

"A ball game."

"I'm not going."

"What's the harm?" Pete touched her arm. "Anyway, you like baseball games."

The harm seemed obvious to her, but the humor in his voice beckoned to her.

"The way I look at it," he went on, sensing her weakening. "If we're with them, their evening is less intimate."

As easily as ever he managed with his logical thinking to say something that seemed ridiculous to her. Ariel laughed. "No one gets intimate at a ball game. And maybe your eyesight is failing you, but they didn't care that we were with them at dinner. He held her hand through the whole meal."

"Hey, you two," Evan yelled out as he pulled the car up next to them. "Come on, or you'll miss the game."

Pete sent Ariel a skeptical look. "My guess is that the score is already in."

Ariel resisted being paired off with Pete. As they strolled with Evan and Virginia past the ticket booth and inched their way toward the bleachers, Ariel stepped away from Pete and closer to her mother. "You were right. Him's was a wonderful place."

Virginia frowned. "You thought so?"

"Yes," Ariel answered brightly. "Good food and—"

"There is no 'and,' Ariel," Pete interjected.

"I like it," Virginia began, "because Evan and I found it together. That makes it special to me."

Evan nodded. "Ginnie and I went there on our first date. It was late in the evening. I had a meeting at school later, so we chose a place close by. After finding Him's," he said, sliding an arm around Virginia's waist, "we thought of it as our place. We'd hoped no one else would find out about it. But they have," he said matter-of-factly.

Ariel exchanged a smile with her mother. "It is different."

"And different is interesting." Pete sidestepped a couple that had stopped in front of him and brought himself close to Ariel again.

The guiding hand on her arm was as firm as the look she'd seen seconds before in his eyes. When he'd spoken those words he'd meant her, not the restaurant. Shivering, she knew she should take his words as a warning to keep her distance. With a look he made her blood rush. With a touch he'd caused her heart to jump once, then thud a little harder, a little quicker. The more time she spent with him, the easier it was to erase years. She didn't want to. She needed to remember the hurt she'd felt when he'd left. If she didn't, the wanting would consume her and lead her on. And if she gave in to it, disaster would strike her heart a second time.

"I'm so glad you both joined us," Virginia said as she stepped to the other side of Ariel. In a stage whisper she added on a sympathetic note, "You've been staying home too much."

Out of the corner of her eye Ariel saw Pete's grin. "Mother, I've gone out several times."

"With whom?"

"I don't ask you that."

"Of course not." Virginia's gaze slid to Evan, who was one step behind her. "You know who I'm seeing." She smiled endearingly at him, then returned her attention to Ariel. "But you haven't gone out enough since your divorce."

"I have."

"Thou dost protest too much."

Ariel groaned, feeling a trap closing in on her. She glanced from her mother to Pete, trying to calculate who was more unsettling at the moment. The answer came swiftly to her as his body brushed hers. She braced herself for sensations, but too many swarmed in on her at once, mingling with an emotion that she'd never manage to ignore. The best she could do was dodge it, not give it a name. But panic wavered beneath the surface, cautioning her that she'd need more than simple evasiveness to resist him.

As she took a seat beside Pete she turned to reason. He used logic to guide his life. So would she, she determined as she promised herself the evening would be lighthearted and casual, and definitely not romantic. If she stayed away from romantic thoughts, she'd be safe.

"Desen is still playing first base?" Pete asked, sounding amazed.

Ariel shifted on the seat next to his, making room as he stretched his legs and angled his feet toward hers. "Why shouldn't he be?"

"He must be forty-two."

"He's the best first baseman the Dukes ever had or ever will have," Ariel countered.

"He should retire."

Evan leaned forward around Virginia and Ariel to see his son. "He hasn't missed a game in twelve seasons."

Beside Ariel, Virginia offered her a bag of peanuts.

Ariel accepted them with a nod, but her thoughts remained on Pete's comment. "If it had been up to you, Moses would have been put out to pasture long before he got the Ten Commandments."

"You're comparing apples and oranges. Desen is an athlete. He needs muscles and stamina."

"Muscles and stamina are needed to climb a mountain."

Amused, Pete watched her struggle with the bag of peanuts. When she began using her teeth to tear it, he extended a hand for the bag. "And to open bags of peanuts," he quipped, splitting the bag for her. Peanuts flew into the air. Though she stifled a giggle, he heard it—a musical sound, airy and bright and contagious.

For a split second he knew they'd stepped back, banished all the years when they'd been apart. Smiling, he handed the bag to her after palming a few.

Ariel stared at the half-filled bag and felt a laugh tickling her throat. This was too easy, she realized, leaning forward and resting her forearms on the railing. First they'd share the bag of peanuts. And then what?

"Desen will strike out," Pete informed her.

She shot a quick frown at him. "What if he doesn't?"

Beneath the gentle summer's breeze strands of hair fluttered across her cheek. "What if he does?" Pete asked, and gently raked the hair away from her face.

A rush of emotion tightened her throat. She fought breathlessness. "This is pointless. You're going to lose."

"You're stalling." He glanced at the field. "Strike one." Leaning forward, too, he rested his weight on one elbow and studied her. Though she was clinging to a serious expression, he saw a hint of a smile tugging at the corners of her lips. "What do you bet?"

"Ball one."

"Come on, Ariel."

She gave in to her mood and faced him with a smile. "If he strikes out, I'll treat you to a movie."

He raised one brow.

Her eyes shot back to the field. "Ball two."

"That's no bet. You're not losing anything. You love the movies."

"One of those terribly depressing kind that you find so thought-provoking."

Pete glanced again at the umpire. "Strike two. And if he gets a hit, I'll take you to one of those ridiculous lighthearted comedies."

"Ball three," she announced, her eyes sliding to him. "I know what you're doing."

Pete laughed. "What?"

"You're not losing."

"How did you reach that conclusion? I hate those slapstick comedies."

"Full count," she said, keeping her eyes on the umpire. She couldn't look at Pete. Old sensations weaved with new ones. They all meant the same thing. She was enjoying herself too much with him, and she knew he was geting to her again with that velvet touch.

Heart pounding, she concentrated on the pitcher, watching and waiting as he wound up, then took the long stride forward, releasing the ball. It spun swift and hard, its whirling motion coinciding with the whirlwind sensation that was making her feel dizzy and light-headed.

Around them the crowd was silent, then a roar rose in response to the ball's exaggerated curve. It whammed into Desen's shoulder, sending him down to his backside.

"He walks," Pete said simply.

Virginia hunched forward to see around Ariel. "Pete," she yelled to be heard over the crowd's indignation, "your father wants to say something."

Both men leaned forward to make eye contact.

Evan grinned. "Desen has the highest statistic for walking this year."

As Pete slanted a look at her, Ariel grimaced.

"You knew that?"

Ariel giggled. "Pete, don't look so offended."

"You knew he wouldn't strike out." A smile touched his lips. "You should forfeit."

"Nope."

He grinned, as enchanted as ever at the sight of her chin raising defiantly. "Why not?"

"It's a bad idea."

"Why is it?"

"Because going to movies with you is the way it all started for us."

He sighed, aware of the uphill battle ahead. "Maybe it will rain."

"What?" Puzzled, Ariel instinctively tilted back her head to look up at the dark sky. Stars sparkled across the black canvas.

"Like your mother said—there's sunshine in the rain. We know that better than a lot of people."

"Oh, Pete—" Ariel shook her head "—you never did play fair."

"Fair doesn't matter. We do," he said softly. "Being together again is what counts."

The roar of the crowd, the sudden excitement in the voice of the announcer, assured her that a batter had hit a home run, but she couldn't take her eyes off Pete's. "It's never been easy with you."

"It's never been easy with you, either." His voice was huskier, intimate. It aroused. It took her back. "But I never asked for easy, Ariel."

She wanted to yell and to laugh at the same time. She wanted to run and to cling. "We wouldn't be together right now if some people hadn't connived," she said, changing the subject so as to stop his softly spoken words. Pointedly she slid a look at Evan and her mother. Blissful, they cheered along with the crowd to encourage the next batter. "I didn't ask to be here," she finally said to Pete.

"But you didn't resist coming," he reminded her. "Think about that. Think about why you didn't."

She knew why. He was the man she wanted to be with. He still meant more to her than any other ever had.

"Drive me to the store," Ariel requested as Pete maneuvered his car away from the long line of vehicles exiting the stadium parking lot.

He glanced at the clock on the dashboard. "Isn't the store closed?"

"Yes, but my car is in the parking lot behind it. And I want to make sure all the doors are locked at the store."

"Your assistant wouldn't do that?"

"Rosie is very conscientious, but I want to double-check."

Pete glanced away from traffic and frowned at her. "Do you always do that?"

"No." Ariel stared out the passenger window to avoid his eyes. Could he hear worry in her voice? She hoped not. She didn't want him prying into her business, asking questions. If he knew about Siske, he'd tell his father, and Evan would tell Ariel's mother.

But would that be so bad? she wondered, wishing she could share the problem with someone. Ariel tugged at a strand of hair. Of course it would be. If her mother learned about Siske, then she'd insist on standing up to him, too. The flower shop meant so much to her. It was a living link to Ariel's father.

Again, Ariel had to consider the risk. If she could avoid jeopardizing the small floral shop that her parents had started when they'd first married, then she would. She wouldn't let her mother lose that after everything else she'd lost, and protecting her meant keeping her plan for Siske to herself.

Pete kept his attention on traffic and his thoughts on her. She wasn't a worrier by nature. She believed that people had to ride the waves in life. So when had she started doing things like double-checking doors? he wondered, noting her white-knuckled grip on the door handle.

"Instead of slowing down our parents' relationship," Ariel said, cutting into his thoughts, "we seem to be pushing them together."

Pete turned down the street that led to her shop. In the distance, like low-hanging stars, lights sparkled around the entrance of a nearby Spanish restaurant. The sounds of the strumming guitars and the melodious voices of a mariachi band traveled on the wind. "I don't see it that way."

"I do. I stopped by to spend the evening with my mother."

He braked the car in front of her shop. "So? I planned on one with my father."

Ariel scanned the storefront, relieved not to see any more broken windows. Assured Siske hadn't returned, she shifted on the car seat to face Pete. "You do realize they manipulated us, don't you?"

Pete's grin widened.

"They planned tonight," she told him.

"How could they have known either of us would have contact with them?"

"They couldn't. But once we did, they set their plan in motion. It's crazy."

"I don't think so."

"I do."

He released a faint, annoyed sigh.

Even in the shadowed light she could see tension tightening his features. "We both learned that opposites attract," she said, wondering how people could love and hurt one another at the same time.

"They do." He swiveled toward her and laid an arm across the back of the seat.

He was studying her, watching too closely. She frowned, eyeing the distance between them. It had shrunk.

"Tell me something." His voice caressed her with its softness. "You really didn't think it was romantic, the way we met?"

He watched as a thoughtful look settled on her face, then changed to a semblance of a smile as she said, "Perhaps it was. But have you forgotten what it was really like? We both looked our worst—sitting in a puddle, our books soaking up water."

"I was sitting in the puddle," he interrupted. "You were on my lap."

Ariel smiled at the memory. Rain had dripped down their faces that day. The warmth and hardness of his body had sheltered her, and the sound of his laughter had mingled with hers. And when her eyes had met his dark ones, dancing with humor, she'd known that he was the one. "Yes, I was," she said softly. Her shoulders heaved as she took a calming breath. Instead of quieting the excitement that the memory had stirred, she inhaled the scent of him. Clean. Soapy. Masculine. As he leaned closer she reached for the door handle. "I'd better go."

He closed his hand over hers, halting her action. "Let's discuss this reasonably."

"Not everything can be explained reasonably or logically. You expect it. I never do."

"I don't always," he said, toying with the collar of her blouse. Was it reasonable that she filled his mind throughout the day? Was it logical that he couldn't love another woman? "Is it logical for a man to send flowers to a woman when he's not sure she won't immediately trash them?''

His breath fluttered across her face. A caress that seemed so real she imagined his touch. "I'd never do that.''

"How could I be sure?''

"The same way that you knew what to wager," Ariel murmured, catching her breath as his fingers brushed the curve of her neck. "You know that I love movies. You deviously—''

He cocked one brow. "Deviously?''

"Yes, definitely, that was devious," Ariel said quickly, deciding talk might be her only defense against her preoccupation with his mouth, the warmth and sweetness that his taste would bring her. "You made the wager something that would please me.''

"How abusive.''

"Yes, you—'' Ariel cut her words short as she considered her side of the argument. Her point of view made no sense.

His fingertips played across the nape of her neck. "Is it out of style for a man to try to please a woman?''

"I doubt it ever will be.''

"Good.'' He leaned closer, letting strands of her hair slip through his fingers, taunting himself with the silky texture that he wanted to bury his face in.

Ariel breathed deeply as his lips moved up her cheek. Her eyes fluttered shut. "Unfortunately you seem overexperienced. It must be a family trait," she whispered, her lashes flickering as his mouth traveled across her cheek to her ear.

"Ah. Turner men are charming, then?''

His lips tickled the shell of her ear, and as his tongue joined the play, her pulse points pounded. Cardiac arrest at twenty-nine, Ariel mused, arching her neck away from the moist heat of his mouth trailing a path down the curve of her neck. "Stuffy," she barely managed to counter.

He nipped her collarbone gently. "What's stuffy about us?"

Ariel struggled to remember the point she'd wanted to make. "You don't have fun."

A chuckle came from deep in his throat. "I disagree."

Her fingers touched the lapel of his suit. As his tongue followed the cord in her neck, she curled her fingers around the cloth. "No one wears a suit to a ball game."

"I was doing my own thing."

His voice sounded thicker, huskier. "Imprinting your own style?" she asked softly.

Gently he nibbled at her jaw. "Making my mark."

Ariel tightened her grip on his lapel.

Pete shifted, fighting a need to rush her. "And if you didn't notice, good old Dad is giving unusual gifts these days. No ordinary things like candy or flowers," he said, burying his fingers in a mass of coppery curls. "Turner men have more imagination."

Didn't she already know that? she reflected. "Do they?"

"Yes, they do."

Ariel slid her hand from his chest to his shoulder. "In what way?"

Pete sighed. She tasted wonderful. She smelled wonderful. She felt wonderful. And he felt weaker, all his senses ganging up on him. Fighting one of them might work. Ignoring all of them seemed like a losing battle. "Balloon," he managed to answer, concentrating on the sweet yet salty taste at her jawline.

Pleasure rippled through her. "He surprised me," she whispered.

"And?"

"He might not be as stuffy as I thought. As stuffy as..."

His mouth taunted the corner of hers. "Don't say it."

"No, I won't," Ariel returned weakly.

He watched her lips part for his. "If I was so stuffy, then why did you live with me for two years?"

"Youthful misdirection?" She felt his smile press against her cheek. "I was bowled over by—"

"My charm?"

"Your intellect."

He moved his mouth closer to hers. "My sensitivity?"

"Your manners."

"My kisses?"

"Your..." His lips brushed hers. "Pete, don't kiss me," she nearly begged.

"Hardly even seemed like a kiss." His lips caressed hers again. "Not like some," he said softly.

A jolt charged through her as his fingers tangled in her hair, and she knew her chance to elude his kiss had escaped her.

"Some linger, drive you crazy so you'll never forget them," he murmured, letting his lips hover near hers. He was driving himself crazy, he reflected.

He was driving her crazy, she mused, tightening her fingers over his shoulders to pull him closer.

His mouth brushed hers, then again, as if testing. As her lips parted he deepened the kiss, silencing anything she might have said.

Ariel didn't care about having the last word. Her hand fluttered, touched his waist, then slowly snaked up under his suit jacket to pull him closer to her. The four years that had passed seemed like four seconds. Sensations so vivid, so right, so familiar, bombarded her.

A soft sigh escaped from her throat as his breath mingled with hers, echoing of the oneness they'd known long ago. Her mouth responded in the way it always had to his sweet, savoring play, to the firm pressure of his lips, to the moist heat of his tongue insisting that hers join in, turning gentleness into hunger.

For four years she'd convinced herself that she hadn't missed him. With one kiss he'd reminded her that she'd never forget him. She felt his hand moving over her, his touch confident, certain that it had a right to caress her softness.

An ache gnawed at her, rising, building with an intensity that frightened her. It, too, was familiar, too familiar. And as her heart pounded and threatened to accompany the racing heat of her blood, she knew she had one more second, one more second of reasoning left in her. If she didn't stop now, she'd be his. She'd be with him once more as if all that pain, all those tears, all those lost dreams, had never existed.

But they had, and they'd happen again if she didn't stop now.

Ariel wrenched her lips from his and turned her face away. She felt the harshness and heat of his breath against the curve of her jaw. She steeled herself, aching to turn her face back to him and struggling not to.

Then she felt him draw away. She wanted to avoid his eyes and couldn't. Moonlight slanted across his face, making it too easy to see his confusion and his pain. They reminded her too much of her own. Quickly she unlocked the door and pushed it open. She needed the crispness of the midnight air. She needed to prevent him from ever kissing her again.

Chapter Seven

She never expected him to follow. So when she heard his footsteps behind her, she quickened hers. As he caught her wrist and stopped her, a breathlessness snatched her energy. She tried to move away, but couldn't. Excitement pumped through her as if she'd been on an amusement park ride. Her bones felt soft, her legs wobbly. She wanted to rest, needed a moment to catch her breath, to slow her heartbeat and regain her equilibrium.

He gave her no time.

He closed his arms around her, drew her to him again. He pressed his lips hard against hers. She felt his anger, the wildness in his mouth twisting across hers. Memories melded with reality. The hunger, the heat, the demand, was real again. The senselessness and the insatiable wanting had returned. A possessive greediness captured them.

Wild now, she sought the taste of his lips, his tongue, the warm recesses of his mouth. She heard the beating drum of her own heart, its rhythm steady as it pumped the blood faster. Her body was hot.

She tried to reason. She was feeling unbalanced by too many memories, she reminded herself. His kisses weren't so great; she only remembered them that way. His taste wasn't the one she'd longed for; she'd only tricked herself into believing that. She wasn't responding; she was dreaming. She'd wake up and realize she was dreaming.

Then she heard his deep moan, felt the heat of his hardness against her, and certainty abandoned her. An unbearable tension took its place. She strained against him, wanting a closeness that wasn't attainable. As if it were years of yesterdays ago, she yearned for the slick texture of his damp skin beneath her fingers. The craving had returned.

She savored all, letting memories and fantasies tumble together. She savored them longer than she knew was wise, then wrestled for the willpower to stop. "Pete..."

He heard surrender in her voice, its softness tangible. Too much that was unsaid, unexplained, stood between them. He could have her, but the open wounds would fester. He stepped back but, aching, he couldn't relinquish his hold on her. He held her upper arms, driven by a need not to lose contact of some sort with her. "Don't pull away. It's right between us. It's always been right."

His fingertips caught her chin and forced her to look at him. She saw longing in his dark gaze. "Pete, I won't pretend," she said breathlessly. "I've always wanted you. I still..." She stopped herself from saying "love." "But none of that matters. We aren't good for each other."

"We're different now."

The roughness in his voice sent a slow-moving shiver up her spine. "No, we're not." Momentarily his grip tightened. Ariel stepped back, forcing him to stretch the distance between them. "Nothing has changed."

"No, nothing has," he answered, knowing he still loved her.

Ariel watched his lips slowly curve into a smile. It used to make her feel good. For no reason, she wanted to smile now.

"You're still stubborn," he said softly. "And so am I. We both always did want everything our own way." He released her while he still could.

At his continued silence she raised her gaze to his. He said nothing, but he looked as if she'd responded to his smile. A shiver passed down her arms, though the wind blew warm as she moved steadily along the walkway that bordered the side of her store. She kept her eyes on her car, which was parked in the lot behind the store, even though she wanted to stop and search his face for reassurance.

"Do you want to check the doors?" he asked.

"Check the doors?"

"Isn't that what you planned to do?"

Blankly, she stared straight ahead for a long second. "Yes, it was." She had to concentrate on something else, anything but him, she reminded herself, turning toward the back door.

As she froze a step from the doorway, Pete quickly joined her. He peered over her shoulder, then reached forward and ran a fingertip across the chipped, jagged edge of splintered wood adjacent to the lock. "Was it like this before?" he asked, inclining his head to see her face better.

Ariel shook her head and began rummaging in her purse for the keys. A dozen questions barraged her mind. Was Siske out of jail? Had he managed to get in? How? If not by the door, then by a window? Before, he'd broken a window to enter the storeroom and steal the crate of gourds. Was he inside now?

Her hand trembled as she retrieved her keys from her purse. Stubbornly she struggled for calm as she shoved the key into the lock.

"Let me go in first," Pete said.

She left him at the door and flew through the shop, flicking on lights, scanning the storeroom and then the front of the shop.

"Damn it," Pete yelled, chasing after her. "Why don't you ever listen to anyone? What if someone—a burglar—had been in here?"

Ariel drew several deep breaths. Nothing had been damaged. Was the jimmied lock just another way for Siske to communicate his threat? "Everything seems okay." She rounded the cash register counter and examined the glass-enclosed case that displayed Italian marble and mother-of-pearl miniature sculptures.

"I'll call the police," he said.

Ariel turned to him. "I'll do it. You can go," she said firmly.

"Go?"

"Leave. I'm fine."

He gaped, then scowled. "You want me to go?"

She knew she was hurting him, rejecting even his desire to stay near, support her, protect her. "You can leave," she said again. "Just lock the door on the way out."

Anger surfaced in him so quickly it nearly rocked him. He couldn't remember the emotion ever having been so intense. "Fine," he spat out.

His eyes gleamed, their hardness reminding her of onyx.

"You're right," he said angrily. "You haven't changed. You're still the most damn stubborn female I ever met." He turned, releasing an explicit oath, and strode toward the door.

Ariel heard the click of the lock in the surrounding silence. She took a step forward, tempted to run and ask him to stay. She wanted and needed him near, but if he stayed she'd drop her guard; she'd welcome him back into her life.

As she pushed the buttons for the police emergency number, she knew of one problem she could eliminate. Earlier she'd planned to tell her mother about Siske. Tomorrow, she promised herself, she'd confront her. Could she do that? she wondered, vacillating again. Of course she couldn't. While Ariel knew enough to bide her time and follow the detective's suggestions, her mother wouldn't. She would plunge in and verbally tackle Siske, not thinking about what his response might be.

"Is there anyone there?" The gruffness of a male voice on the phone assured her that the policeman had repeated himself.

"Yes, I need to talk to Sergeant Hernandez."

"He's not in. What's your name, miss? What's your problem?"

Ariel went through a lengthy explanation and received a promise of a squad car in several minutes. Those minutes seemed like hours before the squad car zipped into the alley.

Ariel calmly waited while the two patrolmen eyed the lock.

"It looks like someone tried to break in," the older patrolman said. His partner nodded.

Ariel counted to ten, striving for patience. "Yes, that's why I called."

"He must have run from you."

"Someone ran from *me*?" she asked, amused and astonished. The idea seemed incredible to her. She assumed they knew the criminal mind better than she did, but she believed that the sight of Pete, not her, had scared off the culprit.

"If you want to leave, we'll stay nearby, keep a closer eye on the store. If he comes back, we'll get him."

Again the younger patrolman nodded.

The idea of her personally standing guard at the shop all night, getting no sleep, and praying no one showed up sounded ludicrous to Ariel. "I'll go home."

"That's good," the older man said in a fatherly fashion. "Get a good night's sleep."

Ariel nodded, thanked them, and walked to her car. Twice she glanced back. Sitting in their squad car, the two officers continued to watch her.

For the first time in her life she understood the cliché "frightened of her own shadow." She checked the back seat of her car before getting in, locked both doors, and spent the next five minutes tensing at every car that pulled up beside her at a red light or stop sign.

Heroism wasn't as easy as the movies made it seem.

Pete tapped an angry beat against the steering wheel of his car. He shouldn't have left her alone. No matter what she'd said, she shouldn't have been left alone.

Pride made people do dumb things, he mused, executing a U-turn. What other excuse did he have for that stupid macho departure? He'd forgotten her unpredictability. Any other woman would have accepted the protective presence of a man, but Ariel never had followed what seemed like acceptable behavior. She challenged; she surprised. She drove him crazy. If he had an ounce of good sense, he'd go home, stay clear of her. But no one ever claimed a man in love acted logically or sensibly.

He drove past the front of her store and rounded the corner to the alley. It was dimly lit. Too dark, he thought, imagining Ariel walking from the storeroom exit to her car. He slowed, then stopped, his curiosity aroused by the faint light shining out of a storeroom window. No true reasoning preceded his cutting off the ignition and getting out of the car. Ariel was obviously gone, but Pete strode toward the door anyway, not considering who was inside until he stood before it.

Financial consultants pushed around pencils, not burglars, he reminded himself. What would he do if he came face-to-face with one? What—

The squeal of tires whirled him around. Headlights glared in his eyes. He raised an arm to shield them, heard the screeching of brakes and running footsteps, and tensed. His muscles bunched, ready to uncoil as he caught the movements of two dark figures. He had no protection but his own fists. Hell of a lot of good they'd be if the guys had guns.

Then he saw the flashing lights on top of the car. One cop was slim, and smaller than he. The outline of the other revealed a heavy man who was older, Pete judged from the lumbering jog.

"Police. Stand still and don't move." The bigger, older one trod closer and recited, "You have the right to remain silent."

"Hey, wait a minute," Pete interrupted, managing a weak smile. "I wasn't doing anything."

The cop continued his recitation as if a recorded message were lodged in his throat.

Pete told himself not to panic. As the smaller cop rushed to stand on the other side of him, Pete nodded. He'd watched enough television cop shows to understand what was being said to him, and to know why. He was a suspect.

"Stand up against the building," the older cop ordered.

"What?" Pete took a step to the side.

The younger one's hand jerked down to his gun.

Pete froze. "Okay, okay." He turned around, spread his legs, and pressed his palms against the wall. Damn, this couldn't be happening to him. He felt one arm and then the other yanked back. Handcuffs were snapped over his wrists.

"What were you doing here?" the older one asked, whirling him around.

"Nothing. My..." Pete hesitated. "I know the woman who owns this store."

"Why were you here?"

Pete released a mirthless laugh. "I wanted to make sure she was all right."

"Why?"

"Someone tried to break in here tonight." Pete started to gesture toward the jimmied lock.

"Don't move," the younger one ordered in a voice that suited his age. "We're taking you to the station."

"I didn't do anything."

The older man propelled him toward the patrol car.

"I know the owner of the store," Pete insisted.

"Fine, then you can call her from the station."

Ariel tried not to think about her mother or Siske or Pete, especially Pete. As she slipped out of her clothes she remembered that she'd left a small light on in a corner of the storeroom. She usually turned out all lights before leaving. Perhaps leaving on a light was best tonight.

She yanked a bright orange, thigh-length football jersey over her head. She knew the color clashed with her red hair. Only the fish swimming aimlessly in the illuminated tank ever saw her wearing it, so she saw no point in switching her loyalty from the Denver Broncos to a team with colors more compatible to her skin and hair color.

For the next few minutes she wandered around, munching on a chocolate bar and blaming the late-night snack on Chinese food.

Finished, she balled the candy wrapper. Restlessness stirred her. On bare feet she padded into the kitchen, tossed the wrapper into the wastebasket, and yanked at the freezer door.

She scooped a second heaping tablespoon of Rocky Road ice cream from its container before her conscience regained control. On a disgusted sigh, she dropped the spoon into the sink. She wasn't hungry; she was nervous. If she wasn't careful she'd gain twenty pounds before she settled all her problems.

Though the situation with Siske threatened her business, her bank account, her mother's business, and maybe even the close relationship she had with her mother, Ariel knew that in time she'd tackle all those problems. They'd be nonexistent worries eventually.

But Pete was dangerous. He'd disrupted her life years ago. Easily, he could do that again.

Ariel slouched on the soft, cushioned sofa and rested her head on the back of it. She closed her eyes. Why hadn't she stopped him from kissing her?

The problem between them hadn't reared its ugly head yet, but if they continued to see each other, eventually the same old conflict would wedge itself between them.

He needed order in his life. He wanted predictability. He thrived on certainties. He cared about the impression he made on others. She didn't suit him, and Jonathan had taught her that she'd smother in a rigid, disciplined life-style.

Pete only thought that they still belonged together. She knew they didn't. Yet when he touched her, her blood pounded and her ears rang. She couldn't think straight. Even now, just remembering those moments, she felt her ears ringing.

Ariel slammed her hands over her ears, but the ringing persisted, demanded attention. Her eyes snapped open. For a long second she stared at the telephone before her mind registered that someone was calling her. On a soft moan, feeling foolish and grateful that she was alone, she reached for the telephone receiver. "Hello."

"Ms. Hammond. This is Detective Sergeant Hernandez."

"Yes."

"I was called a half hour ago. The patrolmen who visited you earlier this evening circled back. They caught a man loitering near your store."

"They caught Siske?"

"I can't say for sure. I know that he did make bail. The patrolmen didn't want to take any chances, so they brought this guy in." Something that sounded like amusement edged his voice. "I haven't questioned him yet."

"But if you caught him trying to break into my store, then I might not have to do anything to stop his extortion. He'd go to jail for burglary, wouldn't he?"

"It's not quite that simple. And he really wasn't caught breaking in. As I said, the patrolmen were a little edgy because they knew about your other problem. If you could come down here and identify the man..."

Ariel shot to a stand and swallowed hard. "Identify him."

"It would help."

"I don't understand. Why would I have to come down and identify him? If he was caught—"

"According to the patrolmen who brought him in, the guy claims he was looking for you."

"For me?" Ariel sat down again.

"This guy claims he knows you. We want to check out his story before we hold him any longer. He said his name is Turner."

"I'll be there in a few moments."

She set down the receiver. "It couldn't be." A giggle bubbled at the back of her throat. "Pete in jail."

She changed quickly. By the time she'd slipped on clothes and sneakers and was grabbing her purse to head for the door, her smile had faded.

Pete was going to be furious.

Virginia handed Evan the egg whisk. "You beat. I'll chop the vegetables."

"Why am I always so hungry after eating Chinese food?"

"Too little dessert."

He cracked an egg before looking back at her. "Would you explain?"

"You get only one little cookie at Him's."

Evan smiled. "That made a great deal of sense, Ginnie."

She juggled a green pepper, onion, and tomato. "Doesn't everything I say?"

"Everything," he assured her.

She set the chopping board on the counter and stood beside him, her face brighter. "They had a good time together. Don't you think so?"

"I don't think we fooled them. Nor am I sure that they had such a good time. They argued."

She stopped slicing a green pepper. "My goodness, Evan, that means nothing. I'd be more worried if they'd acted polite and pleasant. That could mean they no longer feel anything for each other." She resumed slicing. "But now we know that they still care." Turning away, she set a pan on the stove and flicked on the burner. "But I am a little worried. You don't think that I was too hard on Ariel when I mentioned she hadn't dated often, do you?"

"No. She didn't seem upset. But why did you do that?"

Virginia picked up the knife. "To let Peter know that there wasn't another man in her life."

Evan broke another egg. "He knows now. And now, Virginia—"

"Oh, my. When you say Virginia, that always means you're serious."

"I am. I don't think we should meddle anymore."

"No," she said cheerfully. "I don't, either."

"I'd thought you'd argue."

"There's no reason to. Neither of them resisted being together, did they?"

"Perhaps they felt that keeping us from being too lovey-dovey was more important."

"Ariel might consider that, but—" Virginia paused thoughtfully, then shook her head "—no, I don't believe she'd tag along to accomplish such a thing. She went to the ball game to be with him." Virginia held up an onion.

Evan shook his head. "Mushrooms."

She set the onion aside. "I know I'm right about this. They're just being stubborn."

Evan sighed. "But we won't interfere anymore. Isn't that correct?"

"Yes, I agree," she responded. She stopped suddenly, touching his hand. "But that's not what I feel deceptive about."

Evan's eyes met hers. "We've made a decision, then?" he asked, setting down the whisk and facing her.

"We've certainly discussed it endlessly. For now, yes." She sighed on a smile.

"We needed to consider what's best for you and—"

"You," she said softly, framing his face with her hands.

"For now." He looked thoughtfully at her. "For now, we've made the wisest decision." His intention to draw her close came to a jarring halt as the phone rang.

A frown fluttered across Virginia's face. "Who in the world would be calling after midnight?"

Evan shrugged, reaching for the telephone receiver. "Hello. Yes . . . Pete? Peter, it's after— You're where!"

"Is there something wrong?" Virginia asked anxiously, pressing her temple close to Evan's head to hear the conversation.

"But . . . but why?" Evan was saying.

"The police station?" Virginia whispered, her eyes widening.

Evan nodded. "Son, I'll be there in a few— Oh, all right. You'll call me?"

Virginia reached back and switched off the stove burner.

"Son, if you need help, call." He set down the receiver.

"Evan, why is he at a police station?"

"He was cuffed and taken there for trying to break into Ariel's store."

"He did what?"

Evan chuckled. "No, not really. But the police believed he was trying to."

"Oh, Evan, we'd better go." Her gaze darted around the room. "We can leave everything just as it is. I've turned off the stove."

He grabbed her upper arms to stop her whirlwind motion before she flew toward the door. "Don't panic. We don't have to go. Pete said that he insisted the police call Ariel and ask her to come to the station and identify him."

"Oh," she sighed. "Then everything really is all right."

"Yes," he assured her, returning to the bowl of scrambled eggs.

"Well, now." Virginia joined him by the counter. She beamed. "Then we really don't have to do anything else. Everything is happening as I expected it to."

He looked puzzled. "What is happening?"

"Fate steps in, Evan. When two people are right for each other, then fate steps in."

Chapter Eight

Ariol stood in the doorway of the detective's office. Pete's back was to her as he sat in the chair and faced the detective's desk. The light overhead picked up the faint hint of red in his dark hair when he turned to see who had entered the office.

From his profile, she could see his somber expression. The tight pressure around his lips emphasized the high cheekbones, the tense set of his jaw. "Oh, Pete," she said softly, imagining the worrisome thoughts that must be rambling through his head. A financial consultant for the prestigious Bryant and Bryant firm wasn't supposed to get hauled into a police station.

Slowly his head swiveled and he looked back over his shoulder at her.

"Ms. Hammond, you know this man, then?"

Pete's look was deadly.

She directed her attention and her words to the detective, whose expression was definitely friendlier. "His name is Peter Turner. He's . . ."

Pete noted that she hesitated. He'd done the same thing when he'd tried to explain his relationship with her to the two cops earlier.

Detective Sergeant Hernandez smiled. Previously, Pete had thought that the man's broad face was frozen in that deadpan expression. "I see," Hernandez commented.

Ariel opened her mouth to protest whatever he thought he'd seen.

"Can I go?" Pete questioned impatiently.

"Yes, Mr. Turner. I'm sorry we inconvenienced you, but after the attempted break-in at Ms. Hammond's store earlier this evening, we were keeping a close eye on it."

Pete nodded. He wanted more of an explanation, but he wanted the closest exit more. He said nothing until he felt the crisp coolness of the night's breeze flutter across his face. "My car is in the parking lot behind your store. You'll have to drive me there, Ariel."

"Why did you come back?"

He stepped off the curb to cross the street, checking one way, then the other. "I was worried about you. I decided that whether you wanted me there or not didn't—"

"I wanted you there," Ariel admitted softly.

He wanted to smile, to offer her the reassurance she'd refused earlier. He wanted to yell at her and to crush her to him, to demand answers. He wanted to love her. But in the midst of his confusion and conflicting feelings was hurt, so he said nothing.

"I'll follow you home in my car," Pete insisted when ten minutes later she wheeled her car beside his.

Ariel waited in the darkness of the dimly lit alley for the flash of his car's headlights. As she pulled onto the street, his car following, she faced the emotion she'd been dodging since his return. Love. She'd never stopped loving him, and never would. The question of suitability seemed senseless. If getting hurt again was her destiny, then she'd face it willingly this time. She had no choice.

He followed her home, parking his car behind hers. There was no way that he'd leave her side until he had answers. Too much had happened. He walked her to her apartment door, three steps below street level.

Without questioning his actions or her own, she slipped the key into the lock. "Do you need a cup of coffee?"

Pete reached over her shoulder and shoved the door open. "I need a stiff drink."

He trailed behind her, stripped off his suit jacket, and tossed it onto a chair. A wrinkled silk tie tumbled onto the orange, yellow and white throw rug.

Ariel caught the uncertain narrowing of his eyes when he glanced at her sofa. She thought to assure him that it was comfortable, but he took three quick strides and crossed the large room of the three-room apartment. Slowly he began circling the perimeter.

She expected words to pass between them, mostly angry ones, and drew a deep breath preparing for them as she crouched down and reached into a cabinet for a bottle of scotch. The absence of sound stirred her to peek over the counter and see what he was doing. Circling. Or pacing? she wondered, wishing he'd stop moving like some stalking feline ready to pounce on his prey. And why didn't he say something? Why didn't he yell?

Pete wandered the room, dealing with anger, worry, and a driving need to shake her until she explained everything to him. Instead he shoved a fist into his pocket as he stopped beside the illuminated fish tank. "Are they the same fish you had before?"

The chill in his voice made her shiver. "Barney died. Ethel was lonely, so I got Melvin."

Pete peered into the water. "Which one is Melvin?"

Ariel looked up from pouring scotch into a glass. "I don't know. The man in the pet store guaranteed a he. I put the he in the fish tank. From then on they're on their own."

He didn't want to smile. At least not yet. They had some serious talking to do. He turned his back on her again, this time to hide a grin.

The apartment suited her. At ground level, the windows, including a stained-glass one, looked out on a garden of daisies, whose petals were closed for the night. He inclined his head to see into the bedroom. Small, the room contained a bed with a brass headboard and a half dozen rainbow-colored throw pillows. Beside the bed, like a sentry, stood a suit of armor six feet high.

Pete circled the living room again. In a far corner of the adjacent kitchen, bright orange pots and pans hung from a rack above the stove. A white tablecloth embroidered with daisies covered a drafting table. Two unfinished pine chairs flanked it. Near a fluffy, cushioned, multicolored sofa stood a brass replica of a nineteenth-century gas lamppost.

No one but Ariel could blend such a hodgepodge and give it unity. The room was her: warm, bright, and pleasantly different.

Lightly he ran his fingertips across a hand-cranked Victrola. He'd searched all of Albuquerque to find it for her.

At the click of ice cubes behind him, he whirled around, steeling himself to softer feelings as he saw a ruefulness in her eyes. For now, until he got answers from her, he needed control. As she set his glass on the coffee table, he stepped closer. "Tell me what's going on. The police wouldn't have snapped cuffs on me so damn fast if there weren't something more than an attempted break-in being investigated."

Ariel flopped on the papasan chair covered with the same blue-and-orange Persian material as the sofa. He was the last person she wanted to tell about Siske.

The tight clamping of her lips annoyed him. He squelched his temper and sank onto the sofa cushions. Pushing a toe to first one heel of a shoe, then the other, he shoved them off, stretched out his legs, and plopped his feet on the glass-and-wicker coffee table.

She inclined her head. "Comfy?"

"I might on well be. I'm not leaving until you tell me."

"You don't need to get involved."

"I am involved. I nearly got booked this evening. If I knew what was happening in your life, I could have responded intelligently, instead of standing in front of two cops and acting like someone with a brain the size of a quark."

Ariel's brows knit. "Quark? What is a quark?"

"Smaller than an atom."

"Tiny," she agreed seriously, looking down and picking at nonexistent lint on the thigh of her jeans to hide her smile.

He drilled an angry look at her. One way or another, he'd get answers. "Do you have a cigarette?"

"I thought you quit."

"I'm ready to start again," he said distractedly, eyeing a pipe on a display shelf.

Miniatures shared the shelf with the pipe. Tiny replicas of the Eiffel Tower, a Sphinx, the London Bridge, and half a dozen other famous landmarks. He viewed the display as her way of bringing closer to her all the sights she'd longed to see. The pipe was her father's, the man who had shared with her his dream to see the world.

"My father is seeing a lot of your mother," he said. "You're having a lot of problems. Is he in danger being near you or your mother?"

Ariel started to shake her head, but could she honestly say that Evan wasn't? "Pete, I don't think so. My mother isn't even aware of what's going on."

"And what is that?"

Ariel released a long sigh. She had to level with him. "First a crate of gourds was stolen. Then a stained-glass window was broken. Then the gourds were returned, all smashed. A note accompanied them. 'Notice two—premium due. I'll be back.'"

Pete frowned.

"A man came in and told me that he would be collecting the premium payments."

Pete leaned forward, anger churning within him as the underlying meaning of her words sank in.

"He wanted money for my mother's store and mine, or he'd do more damage. I've talked to other store owners. They've been visited by him, too. Most of them are too scared to do anything."

Pete tensed inside. He didn't like this. Damn, he definitely didn't like the sound of this at all. He knew her too well.

"I went to the police and talked to Detective Hernandez," she told him.

"You said that your mother doesn't know."

"No."

"Why not?"

"Because I don't want her involved. She and my dad struggled to start that flower shop. It's all she has left of what they'd shared. I don't want to see her lose it."

"You should tell her," he said.

"I've had a similar argument with myself, but I'm not sure what she'd do if she knew." Ariel sighed. "I know she wouldn't let me handle this alone."

"You're not alone. I'll help you."

Ariel shook her head, avoiding his eyes. "The police are going to help. We're working out a plan to catch him."

"We're? You and them?"

She didn't answer.

"What are you going to do?"

"I don't know yet." She pushed herself out of the chair and hurried to the refrigerator. Her mouth felt dry as she began to consider what she might have to do. For all her bravado, she was scared. She poured herself some orange juice and took a long swallow. "I'm not really alone. I'm helping the police."

Frustration snapped his anger. He rushed to his feet and crossed the room to stand behind her. "Forget them. They'll protect, but they won't ache inside if something happens to you. I will," he said on a hard breath.

His words stunned her, snapping her tenuous control. She stared at the liquid in the glass, not able to face him, certain that if she did, he'd convince her of anything. "What do you suggest I do? Pretend he never came to see me? I'm an optimist, Pete. That doesn't mean I believe life is a fairy tale." She turned on the spigot to rinse the glass. The sound of rushing water relieved the heavy silence that hung like a thick barrier in the space between them. "No knight is going to slay the dragon for me."

He suddenly touched her shoulders and turned her to face him. He held her, unable to ignore the slight tremble he'd heard in her voice. "You don't need to slay any dragon alone. Together. We'll slay him together," he told her, wanting to protect her. He felt the heat of her hands on his back. It seemed like forever since he'd held her in his arms in a comforting way, since he'd felt that she'd wanted to be close to him. One kind of tension slipped away as another kind took its place. With every breath he drew, her scent intoxicated him a little more. For the moment he was satisfied with only holding her. For the moment.

She released a long breath. "If we fail . . ."

He knew she was talking about them and not some symbolic dragon in her life. "No." The word was torn from his throat. "Don't think about that," he insisted in a fierce whisper.

As she tilted her head back to look at him, his gaze followed the creamy flesh that narrowed at her throat and disappeared under the pale blue cloth of her blouse. Slowly he undid the buttons of her blouse, exposing the lace of her camisole, the swell of her breasts. The pale peach silk rippled under his hand as he touched her waist. He remembered the flesh, softer than any fabric, that hid beneath the cloth.

Ariel swayed against him, lured by his soft, gentle, undemanding kisses tracing the curve of her jaw. Neither impulse nor lust led her. Love controlled her simplest response to him. A sigh against his lips. A shiver from the warmth of his knuckles brushing against her flesh as he slid her blouse from her shoulders. A need nurtured by memories and aroused by sensation as he slipped a finger beneath the strap of her camisole.

Whispery kisses became deeper ones. She tasted a promise and a demand, a wild insistence that she'd known before and craved for too long. His tongue teased hers, first lazily, then hungrily. Lips clung and bruised. Her world tilted. When had they moved? she wondered as he braced his arm against her back and she sank onto the soft mattress. What did it matter? She'd acted on impulse most of her life. But no whim urged her now. With a need so strong that its ache curled her toes, she lifted first one shoulder and then the other to aid him in sliding the camisole down.

She couldn't speak, only listen. She heard the thunder of her own heart, the soft, intimate tone of his voice as it enticed and urged. She no longer could think. Her mind focused only on the memory of the wonderful days and nights during the best years of her life.

Warmth and cold mingled within her as he shifted, shrugging off clothes from himself, easing them from her. A wanting she'd thought she'd never feel again returned when the smooth, hard length of his body rested against hers.

The magic of their first time echoed in the quickening of their breath. Murmured words blended and tongues touched, tantalizing and tasting.

"Too long," Pete whispered. His gaze met hers for one heart-stopping second. He saw a reflection of the passion and love he felt. Again his lips brushed hers, then found her breast, and with each breath he took, he absorbed more of her. He taunted. He pleased. His mouth lingered and persuaded until he heard her moan at the rush of pleasure engulfing her.

Her excitement fed his. He moved lower, his hand following curves, memorizing the softness that equaled no other. She was wild beneath his hands. He was lost beneath hers. He yearned to savor and rediscover every sensation of his every touch on the angles of her body, but a searing heat rippled through him as her fingers grazed his hips and then his thighs. She swept away his control with a caress lighter, airier, than the brush of a butterfly's wing. As her strokes turned swifter, his grew more urgent. Need took possession with its inescapable force. He lowered his head and filled himself with the taste of her, greedy for the sweetness only she possessed.

The touch of his fingers, the moist path of his tongue, whirled her into another world. Dark, wild, and encompassing. And as pleasurable torment greeted her, a passing of yesterdays and a lifetime of tomorrows flashed before her, brightened by the glow of lights. Then he closed his mouth over hers again and tugged her to him, desire enslaving both of them. Restraint leashed for years broke loose when he entered her, his flesh flowing into her flesh, his heart becoming hers.

A turbulence as fierce as a tidal wave flowed over them. It offered no coolness. It lapped like fiery tongues. Madness accompanied it. Stunning, driving madness.

Sanity crumbled. The world dissolved until only they existed. Her mouth clung to his until a breathtaking urgency rushed fast and furious through both of them.

Desperation coiled around her and she arched against him, flesh warming flesh. Tenderness was forgotten, abandoned as impatience overwhelmed them. She welcomed it, following him, matching him, leading him.

Together again as one, they conquered; they surrendered. They clung, drawing strength from each other. And time passed without measure, promising a lifetime of tomorrows.

A forever time absent of sight and sound drifted over them as they remained in an embrace of tangled arms and legs.

Later, curled into him, her body damp and flushed, she kept her eyes closed and listened to his breathing, which was no longer harsh or quick. A contentment she hadn't felt in years settled over her.

Shifting, she gazed up at him. "Rain," she whispered. "Do you hear the rain?"

Pete squeezed his eyes closed tighter, not ready to open them and lose the sensations that darkness offered. "Nice sound," he murmured, listening to the beat, which was quick and steady.

She laughed softly. "I'm glad it rained tonight."

Lightly he ran his fingers up and then down her arm to meet her hand. She clasped her fingers with his as he shifted to his side and curved her softness against him.

Ariel raised her head and saw that he was now looking at her. In the shadowy darkness of the room his eyes were so intense, so exciting, that emotion constricted her throat. "I've missed you," she whispered, resting a hand on his cheek. Slowly her tongue met and then glided over his. She sighed, giving in to the fire blazing through her as she felt his hands slip between her thighs.

Pete closed his eyes again, losing himself to the moment, wanting a lifetime of moments like this one. As she slid onto him, taking control this time, his thoughts fled. His feelings dominated, consuming him. The rain pounded harder, accompanying the beat of his pulse when her thighs gripped his hips, offering with her pleasurable warmth both madness and serenity.

Ariel awoke to the soft patter of a drizzle. She snuggled closer to Pete. She wondered if it was conceivable to be ecstatic and worried at the same time. Was she experiencing both those emotions, or was she insane? A little insane, probably, she decided. Insane with love and unsure of love's power to withstand conflict.

At the memory of years of torment she scrambled from the bed, pushing away her morose ponderings, which would dull the joy she was feeling.

Standing by the window, she cocked back her head to look up at the sky. Sunshine streaked out from behind a drifting, dark cloud. In a few minutes the moisture on the grass would gleam beneath the sun's brightness.

Turning, she leaned back against the window frame and watched him. His breathing was slow and steady. Would it be different this time? Were they being given a second chance? As she did with all things, she grabbed the emotion of the moment and clung to it. Because happiness dominated, she followed that mood, ignoring any other.

On a pleased sigh, she grabbed the football jersey and tugged it over her head. As the cloth slid around her hips, she glanced at the clock on the bedside table. Sometime during the night, he'd set the alarm. Ariel peered at the setting. In minutes the high-pitched buzzer would go off. He'd moan, reach out, jab a finger at the snooze button, and bury his head under a pillow for another five minutes. Routines ruled his life.

She had five minutes before he'd bound from bed, his actions as quick and decisive at six in the morning as they were at six in the evening. He'd shower and dress in silence until he'd consumed two cups of coffee.

She padded into the kitchen and plugged in the coffee-brewer. One night, she reflected, and the past four years seemed nonexistent. She felt no strangeness, no anxiety at what she'd say to him during the first strained moments of the morning after. She knew better than to say anything to him until he was fully awake.

Pete shifted on the bed, stretching his legs. They made no contact with the slim, warm ones that had tangled with his during the night. Eyes still closed, he moved his hand across the sheet, searching for her. Then he heard the sounds from the kitchen. This hadn't been a dream.

Fantasies sometimes blended with reality. He'd known again all of her sweetness. He'd felt her gentleness, her gift for giving and sharing that surpassed what he'd known with any other woman. And he smiled, keeping his eyes closed, and knew that this time would be forever. It had to be, he realized, or he'd die without her.

The coffee-brewer hissed loudly in a duet with the shrilling buzz of the alarm. Both sounds cut off at the same time.

Ariel flung open the refrigerator door. A quart of orange juice, a pitcher of green Kool aid, a brick of cheese, and a jar of peanut butter. She pondered the selection, wondering how he felt about peanut butter and cheese on crackers for breakfast.

Pouring two cups of coffee, she listened for the rush of water from the shower. Silence prevailed. Curious, she wandered back into the bedroom with two cups in her hands and was surprised to see him still in bed. "Pete?"

He opened one eye. In his peripheral vision he caught sight of the armored sentry that stood guard over her bed.

Ariel hesitated, then took her life in her hands and decided to talk to him. "You used to jump out of bed."

He thought she looked adorable wearing a bright orange football jersey, her hair tousled. "Still do."

"What happened this morning?" she asked, not believing he hadn't grunted a response at her.

As she sat on the side of the bed, he let his fingers skim the side of her knee and thigh.

"Never mind answering," she countered, offering the cup to him. "Drink this first."

"You're too far away," he mused, noting her back-side on the edge of the bed. He pushed himself up and jammed a pillow behind his back.

She followed the urge of his hand at her waist. When he lifted the sheet in invitation to her, she set down her cup. The arm that was curled around her tightened and pulled her close beside him.

"I told you I've changed," he said between sips of his coffee. "I'm coherent now without caffeine."

"Hmm. This is nice," she whispered, shifting her head to find the familiar spot on his shoulder.

"Better than nice. Much better." He kissed the bridge of her nose. "Why did you buy these sheets?" he asked, running his foot across the fresh crispness of the cloth.

She smiled, closing her eyes. "Not too many people want Snoopy sheets for a queen-size bed."

He nuzzled her neck. "Did you get any Charlie Browns?"

"Every single one of them. I knew a man—" she said, bending her head and kissing his chest with fluttery kisses, "—who loved Charlie Brown sheets."

"Sounds like a silly man," he said thickly, aware of the heat that was tightening his stomach muscles.

"Occasionally," she murmured. Urged on by the sudden quickening of his heart, she trailed hot kisses down to his belly. "He made me laugh."

Consumed with desire, the heat of her breath on his skin made him tremble. He'd forgotten that with her hands she could render him helpless in seconds. He'd forgotten the wanting her mouth stirred within him. A powerful desire weakened and strengthened him. Greedily his hand cupped the soft roundness of her hip. "He will again," he promised on a quick breath. Slowly he skimmed her hip, then hooked a finger beneath the hem of her jersey and raised it. "I love you. I want you here beside me. Every morning," he said softly, "for the rest of our lives."

This, then, was the reason for her worry, Ariel realized. He treated nothing casually. She knew that about him. He committed himself firmly and quickly. She loved that trait in him, but she also wanted not to see it displayed this morning.

"Hey." He touched her hair, pushing it back so he could nibble at her ear. "Where are you?" Very gently, he kissed the shell of her ear again.

"With you," she admitted on a sigh.

He laughed and pulled her closer against him. "Did you hear me before? I want you here forever." Pete tightened his hold instinctively as he felt her body tense. "We were younger, Ariel," he said quickly, sensing her resistance. "I wanted one thing. You wanted another."

She wished for an easy answer. "Pete, I still make rash decisions. I act impulsively."

"I know all that." He scooted down and pressed his mouth against her collarbone.

"You'll worry," she said. "I'll want to tread out on the tightrope, and I will, and you'll stay back and check it first for a net." She drew a long breath, her stomach muscles tightening in response to his lips' descent.

"I'll be there with you this time," he whispered, his breath hot and quick against her.

Like a butterfly's caress, his lips grazed her flesh. A slow-moving chill swept over her as he slid his hands beneath the jersey and gently pulled it up and over her head. Tenderly he let his hand skim her waist and hip with a feather-light touch. His lips teased the curve of her breast while his fingers danced across her thigh.

As he lowered his head, his tongue slowly trailing the same path as his hand, Ariel couldn't think of one reason why she and Pete didn't belong together. With the experienced touch of someone who knew the secrets of her body, he lured her into a world she'd journeyed to before and longed to travel to again with him, always with him, only with him.

A brightness that equaled the sun broke through and blazed down on her. She shuddered, unable to think about anything but the intense force driving through her. Tomorrows no longer mattered. She wouldn't, couldn't, think about them, she realized as she let her hands glide over his arms and his back, feeling the smoothness and heat of his flesh. Urging him, she clutched at his shoulders.

As he poised over her and stared down, his dark eyes mirrored the emotion cascading through her. Then she opened her body to him, and when he entered her, she knew they'd only just begun—again.

Chapter Nine

Pete eyed the clock on the wall behind Muriel's desk. "The clock is fast," he said to her bent head as he strode past her.

She didn't look up. "No. You're late."

"I'm never—" He cut his words short and shoved back his cuff to glance at his watch. He was late. He stopped dead in his tracks, then laughed, amused and amazed. "Guess so. Call the deli down the street and order a Danish, will you?"

"Late and no time for breakfast?" Muriel still didn't raise her head, but he saw one pale brow shoot up.

"Only peanut butter cookies," he said lightly, letting his mind drift to those moments with Ariel when he'd stood in the kitchen doorway and watched her rummage through her cupboards. Her list of staples would have made any junk-food addict ecstatic.

"...appointment with Carol Jamison. And J.C. called five minutes ago."

Pete snapped himself back to his surroundings. "Bryant called?" Frowning, Pete contemplated a reason for the unexpected call. "Okay, get him for me."

"You want to talk to him now?" Muriel questioned. "Ms. Jamison is due here any minute."

Pete blew out a long breath. He'd forgotten the appointment. In his present mood he wished he could cancel it. He wasn't ready to talk to her or J.C. "No, she'll be here for the morning only. I'll return his call after she leaves."

Pete settled behind his desk and restacked several manila file folders, then shuffled them again.

Business was the last thing on his mind. That surprised him since he liked his work. At times he'd acknowledged to himself that he'd been a workaholic, but not this morning. Good feelings sprouted from an intangible source. In another room the ticker-tape machine hummed continuously, but his attention was focused on a crow outside his office window.

A late summer's breeze swayed petals of bougainvilleas. Perched on a tree limb near them, the crow rubbernecked, then parted its beak. Pete listened hard for its caw. Faintly he heard it and another answering from farther away. The bird lifted its head, spread its dark wings, and rose, circling back to the tree. Pete bent forward to see where the crow had landed. It teetered on a limb a close but comfortable distance from a smaller and less majestic bird. "You and me, pal," he mused. "You're probably supposed to be building a nest somewhere. Instead you're playing hooky."

For the next thirty minutes he stared down at a client's financial statement, but his mind rejected thoughts about blue-chip stocks, T-bills, and mutual funds. He thought of rain and Snoopy bedsheets and peanut butter cookies. He thought of Ariel: her scent, her taste, her softness. He thought of playing hooky, too.

A permanent ache had settled inside him. Strong and intense, it had kept him awake during the nights when he wasn't with her, and now it haunted him during the daylight hours. There was only one cure, and only the future would reveal whether he'd find it or not and whether the love she felt for him equaled his for her.

For the next hour Carol Jamison rifled questions at him. She was a quick-paced interviewer. Her questions were direct and pointed, indicating she valued his time and her own.

Though confident he'd answered her questions with sufficient intelligence for her to give him a good write-up, Pete wanted the interview to end. As she wound up their conversation, sprinkling in pleasantries about the weather, a tinge of impatience made him eager to escort her out the door.

Concern for Ariel consumed him. Why hadn't he talked more to her about the extortionist? Where was she right now? Had she been contacted by him? Why hadn't he insisted on a promise from her that she wouldn't do anything about the extortionist unless Pete was around?

"Mr. Turner?"

Pete blinked and refocused on the woman sitting across the desk from him. Her look was a questioning one.

As she repeated herself, she scanned the plaques on his walls. Achievement plaques awarded to him because he'd kept his mind on business, he reflected, and focused on fielding her last few questions. While she jotted down notes on a steno pad, the door was still opening.

Muriel buzzed him. He picked up his phone. "Yes?"

"Be careful," Muriel whispered.

"Thanks." Pete frowned, hanging up. What the devil was she trying to alert him to?

"Though this is all really interesting..." Carol Jamison's gaze shifted to the clock on his desk. "I'm running late." She gave him a semblance of a smile. "Another interview."

Pete pushed back his chair and stood expecting her to stand. Instead she remained seated.

Pen poised in her hand, she looked up at him questioningly. "Could you clarify one thing for me before I leave?"

Pete offered a polite smile.

"Is it the usual policy of Bryant and Bryant to offer services beyond the stated ones?"

Pete tensed. "It's my turn to request clarification."

"Were you at a client's store—the Potpourri Bazaar—last night when the police picked you up for attempted burglary?"

She studied him in a measured manner. The look annoyed him. He eyed the upright pen in her hand and chose his words carefully. "The police made a mistake."

She flipped back several pages in her notebook. "According to a Detective Hernandez no charges were filed against you. Yet—" she paused to study him "—that doesn't explain what you were doing in a dark alley after midnight at the back entrance of a store."

Pete plastered a controlled, noncommittal smile on his face. "No, a police report wouldn't explain that. How did you hear about this?"

"A friend of mine works on the newspaper's crime beat. Your PR man in New York stated that you'd undoubtedly have a good reason."

Pete swallowed a fierce curse over the fact that she'd called the New York office and questioned the people there. Was that why J.C. Bryant had called before nine in the morning? Had he been contacted, informed that the company's sterling image was being threatened by one of their up-and-coming junior associates?

She continued. "They insisted that in the fifty-seven years since J.C. Bryant Senior opened the doors, the firm's employees have always epitomized scrupulous behavior in all facets of their lives. To believe otherwise was unthinkable."

Pete strolled around the desk to the office door. "They're absolutely right." He flung open the door.

As she joined him on the threshold, he spoke loud enough to cue Muriel for help. "If neither of us had an appointment, we could discuss this further. However..."

Muriel bounded from her chair to rescue him. "Excuse me, Mr. Turner, but Mr. Doright requested a slight change in plans. He'd like you to meet him in five minutes."

Pete feigned an anxious glance at the clock on the wall. Frowning, he looked back and met Carol Jamison's scrutinizing gaze. She might guess that she was being manipulated, but at the moment all he cared about was getting her to leave. "I'll barely make that meeting in time, Ms. Jamison," he said, turning back toward his office. "We'll discuss that matter further tomorrow. I have to hurry. Excuse me," he called out before closing the office door and releasing a long breath.

Muriel deserved a raise. He'd take care of that after he decided what he was going to say to J.C. Tomorrow he'd handle Jamison and if he was careful, what else could possibly go wrong? Plenty. Ariel complicated his life;

that hadn't changed. She also made it more interesting. When she was near, he wavered between exasperation and laughter. When she touched him, he stood in a chill and felt his blood warm. When she smiled, he struggled for logic and dreamed of love.

"Close call," Muriel quipped from the doorway, jarring Pete back to the present.

He smiled gratefully at her. "You're quick on your feet, lady."

She examined her nails, then buffed them on her lapel. "A genius," she responded unabashedly.

Pete laughed. "Agreed."

"Now, fill me in." Inquisitiveness sparkled in her eyes. "Never before have I known anyone who's been in jail," she said. "How was it?"

"I wasn't in jail. They held me until Ariel came and identified me."

Muriel's hazel eyes twinkled. "A woman got you out of jail. Did she get you into it, too?"

Pete sat back on the edge of his desk. "How did you know what happened?"

"While you were in here with Carol Jamison, Arlene called me."

"Who's Arlene?"

"A friend of mine. She works in the accounting department at B and B's New York office."

Pete moaned. "Does everyone in the world know?"

"Everyone at B and B does," Muriel informed him.

"Including J.C.," Pete said with certainty. "Who originally hired you, Muriel?"

"J.C. himself."

"Does he know you bet on horses?"

She winked. "Ten to one, he'd turn beet red if he knew. Why are you asking? Have you decided to turn me in?"

"Do I look insane?"

"Need me?"

"Desperately. If you were a few years younger and I were a few older..."

"You'd still be in love with the lady who sprang you last night."

Pete laughed easily. "You're a good guesser."

"Not this time. Reason, not risk, led me to that conclusion. Of all the junior associates at B and B, you're the one who has the shiniest reputation. If you got in a little mischief, then a woman was involved."

He frowned suddenly. "What do you think J.C.'s reaction is going to be to my little escapade?"

Muriel curled her lip in a sneer.

"That bad?"

She leaned back against the wall and took a comfortable stance, a signal to Pete that he was about to hear another one of her stories.

"About ten years ago I was working in the typing pool—a gossipy group. I heard a story that J.C.'s father fired a woman after someone showed a photograph of her in a bathing suit."

"Too brief?"

"It didn't reach her knees."

Pete chuckled. "Are you enjoying yourself at my expense?"

"Not me," she said innocently, heading for the door. "But when you worry, you brood," she added. "I used to love the way Gregory Peck brooded. Made me swoon." She stopped in the doorway. "Do you want me to call Mr. Bryant's office for you?"

"Might as well. And afterward," he teased her, "I'll brood and you swoon."

Pete finished his explanation to J.C. and waited. The silence stretched, making him feel like a condemned man. Anxiously, Pete shifted the phone receiver to his other hand, yanked at his tie and opened the top button of his shirt.

Fortunately, Bryant cleared his throat then. "As I see it, Turner, your intentions were misunderstood."

"That's right, sir."

"And this woman who owns the store. If she were gray-haired and needed protection, then some of our more conservative clients would be understanding, since they are among the octogenarian set. Is she gray-haired?"

"No, she wouldn't fit that description."

"Hmm. Too bad. *Ariel Hammond.*" He said her name as if it were foreign and strange to pronounce. "Ariel? Peculiar name. What kind of business does she have?"

"She sells imports."

"She's not a Communist or a smuggler, is she?" he asked gruffly.

Pete nearly laughed. "No, she isn't."

"Image is extremely important, Peter."

J.C.'s use of his first name relaxed Pete, but a surge of resentment crept over him. He'd met his share of other associates' wives. Some weren't lily-white models of society, just discreet, and none of them possessed a thimble's worth of the warmth and caring that Ariel offered.

Although he had no reason to feel hostile, he could not subdue his sudden instinct to protect her. Bryant wasn't attacking her. He was merely discussing a corporation in need of reorganization for tax purposes. Pete struggled to listen to him.

Shafts of afternoon sunlight lightened the room by the time he finished the conversation. He set down the receiver, then spat out a curse as the light on his phone flashed with another call. Somehow he managed not to bark a hello.

"Pete, it's Dad. Could you stop by my place tonight?" Evan said without the usual pause for more greeting.

Pete rubbed his fingertips across his forehead. Everything seemed a touch off kilter to him, even his own father. "If you're concerned about what happened last night, everything is all right now."

"Good, son. But there's something else I need to talk to you about. It's important."

"If you have a problem..."

"Pete, you always expect the worst. You have to learn to view life through a brighter lens. Nothing is wrong," Evan assured him. "Come about seven. Virginia will be here, and she's called Ariel and invited her, too."

Pete didn't question his father further. He'd already guessed what the important news was. So they were going to announce that they planned to get married, he mused. A week ago he'd have been upset. But why shouldn't his father be as susceptible to the Hammond charm as he was?

If Virginia made his father happy, then she was right for him. But... Always there was a but.

Pete reached into a bottom desk drawer and pulled out a pack of cigarettes. He fondled the unopened package, then tossed it back into the drawer. He wished he could discard his worry for his father with the same ease.

One woman had ripped Evan apart. Pete knew now that his mother had never intended to hurt anyone, but when she'd left him and his father, she'd upset not only their personal lives but also his father's career. She'd left because she was bored; that's what she'd told him years later. After all those years, she'd wanted to experience something new, so she'd abandoned her marriage and a career. What if Virginia learned after marrying him that his life was too mild, too calm, too predictable, to suit her? Would she, too, leave?

Ask yourself the same questions, he reminded himself. What about Ariel? She was her mother's daughter. Divorced, she claimed that she'd sampled his type of life while married to Wessell. She hadn't liked it.

Frustrated, Pete passed a hand through his hair. He wasn't Wessell, and what he and Ariel shared wasn't dull or boring. It never had been and never would be. She saw a superficial similarity between him and Wessell. They weren't the same kind of men. Pete loved everything about her that Wessell had wanted to stifle. He drew a long breath, wondering if he'd been unfairly comparing surface similarities between his mother and Virginia. He had no way of knowing; only time would answer that.

Virginia flung open the door and beamed at Ariel. "You came earlier than I expected."

"Not too early."

"No, dear. I'm glad you did. It gives us time to talk. Let's go into the kitchen. I love Evan's kitchen," she said. "It's so warm and cozy."

Ariel followed, passing through the neat rooms that were filled with Early American furniture. "Why did you ask me to meet you here?"

Virginia kept walking and waved a hand back at her. "Oh, we'll discuss that later. Come," she urged. "Sit at the kitchen table." Quickly she poured coffee for each of them and set cups on the calico placemats. Joining Ariel at the round oak table, she asked, "Tell me what happened yesterday at your store. Why did the police arrest poor Peter?"

"They didn't arrest him. He was taken to the station for questioning."

"Evan explained all that, but I still don't understand why the police didn't just ask Peter a few questions and let him go."

Nervously, Ariel rubbed a hand across her flowery skirt. All day she'd argued with herself about whether or not to tell her mother about Siske. *Do it now*, she thought. *Right now. Tell her now.* "You know that I contacted the police."

"Yes, that's what Evan explained, but he didn't know more than that. Peter simply said that the police were jumpy because of an earlier call."

"Someone tried to break into my store yesterday evening."

Distress settled on Virginia's face. "Was anything stolen?"

"No. Nothing."

"You mean the police surprised the burglar?"

"No, he jimmied the lock but never got in."

Virginia pressed fingertips to her lips and stared thoughtfully at Ariel. "Oh, no. Ariel, what is going on? Is someone trying to force you to sell?"

Ariel blinked. "What did you say?"

"Well, someone must be deliberately doing these things to you."

"You don't think it's a burglar?"

"Nonsense. A burglar breaks in quickly and quietly, steals what he wants and leaves. He certainly doesn't try to enter by a stained-glass window that's seven feet high. And he doesn't break into a shop that carries mother-of-pearl and Italian marble to steal a crate of gourds. And the back lock on your storeroom is quite easy to jimmy."

"It is?"

"Yes, I meant to tell you about that but I forgot. Last week or the week before," she said, shaking her head. "I'm not sure when exactly. But I'd forgotten a bag of wigs for the play. I'd picked them up. You know we all have to do more than act to make the play successful, so I volunteered to get the wigs. I'd left them in your store by accident. I think that was two weeks ago," she said with more certainty. "Well, when I remembered them, you'd already left for home. So I slipped a credit card into the back door lock."

"And opened it?"

"Yes, it was quite easy."

Ariel shook her head. "Where did you learn that?"

"Oh, I think anyone who watches television gets a few tips on successfully leading the life of crime."

Ariel laughed. "I suppose you're right."

"So back to what we were discussing. Do you think someone is trying to force you out of business, or do you think this is that grubby little man's handiwork?"

"What grubby little man?"

"Now, let me think." She looked up at the wallpaper, which was decorated with teapots and daisies. "Cyst? No, that's wrong. S-s..."

"Siske?"

"That's right," Virginia said.

"What do you know about Siske?"

"Have you heard about him, too?"

"Who told you, Mother?"

"Why, Mrs. Tremble. She's so frightened of that man. He came to her store and threatened her and Mr. Tremble. I told her that she should go to the police. She wouldn't hear of it. Quite honestly, Ariel, I've been concerned. I thought it was a matter of time before we were contacted by him. But surprisingly, he hasn't yet."

In a way, Ariel reflected, part of Virginia Hammond's charm was the innocence of her manner. It fooled people sometimes. Even her own daughter, or Ariel wouldn't have underestimated her mother's intelligence. "Yes, he has."

Virginia's blue eyes rounded. "Oh, my. So he's the one who's been doing all this to your store?"

Ariel nodded. "And I went to the police."

"I knew I raised an intelligent child."

Ariel smiled.

"What did they say we should do about him?"

"They said that they'd tell *me* what to do."

The corners of Virginia's mouth turned down in a disapproving look. Ariel squirmed. How did her mother manage to unnerve her without saying a word? she wondered, feeling closer to ten than thirty.

"Ariel, I rarely offer advice, because you never listen to it."

"But I do," Ariel protested.

"If I'm saying what you want to hear, but I insist you listen this time. I suffered with you through a week and a half of chicken pox. I made fifteen pink-and-lavender elephant costumes for your Brownie troop. I relinquished the family garage to thirty teenagers while they built a homecoming float. So I certainly am due a request of my own. I am not going to let you do this by yourself."

"I didn't think you would," Ariel answered. "Why didn't you say anything about Siske before this?"

"I know you, dear. If I had said anything, you'd have jumped in to help." Virginia bounded from the chair and reached into a cabinet for an apple-shaped cookie jar. "Remember your campaign to save the koala bears? And as a child, you led your class to stop that new principal's weekly locker inspection. You declared that it was an invasion of privacy. If there's the vaguest hint of an injustice, you battle it. You're quite predictable, Ariel."

Ariel stared dumbly at her. She was predictable? All her life she'd believed she acted on whims, impulsively charging into a situation, but even that had been done with a consistency, she realized now. In his own way had Pete, with his analytical grasp of things, seen and understood that? Did Pete, unlike Jonathan, accept her predictable quirks?

Virginia set a plate of cookies on the table. "We must of course..."

"Not we. Me." Ariel poked a finger at her chest. "And I have plenty of help. Pete knows, and he insists on helping. And the police know, so they'll help me. All you have to do is let me know if Siske contacts you."

"Are you sure that you don't want me to do anything else? I know a florist who has a Venus's-flytrap. We could set it outside the walkway, and when he comes close, it would..." She slapped her hands together.

Ariel giggled. "No, let's not do that."

Virginia smiled with her. "I thought not."

Ariel shifted on the straight-backed chair, which was padded by a thin seat cushion. Evan's home was the home Pete had been raised in. Though homey and warm, the subtle decor reflected traditional values and old-fashioned ideals. She believed in those, but she knew that sometimes they smothered free expression. She'd always thought Pete—the public Pete, anyway—was a little uptight. Looking around the room, she could imagine the quietness that had surrounded and molded him.

As if it were the first time she'd been there, Virginia said softly, "I've always liked the kitchen in Evan's house. It's very secure."

Ariel sipped coffee. "Where is Evan?"

"He had to rush to the store. He wanted to celebrate, and he said that no one could celebrate without champagne."

"What are we celebrating?"

"Why I can't tell you that. Evan will." Virginia beamed. "Ariel, you haven't learned patience yet, have you?"

"I'd like to know what's going on. Especially if it involves you."

Virginia touched her hand. "Of course you do. Just as I want to know what's happening in your life." She scooted her chair closer. "Such as, what is happening between you and Peter?"

Ariel frowned. "I'm not sure."

"Are you being evasive?"

"No, Mother, I really don't have anything to tell you. I don't have any answers."

"That happens sometimes in life. And then poof—" Virginia snapped her fingers. "Just like that, all the answers come."

"Is that what happened to you?" Ariel asked, trying to find out if the celebration was to announce an engagement.

"Why, yes, I guess that is what happened." She nudged the plate of cookies toward Ariel. "You should eat more. You're looking thin."

"Mother, you saw me yesterday. We ate dinner together. How could I look thinner today?"

"I don't know, but you look thinner." Her blue eyes fixed on Ariel's. "Perhaps it isn't that you look thinner.

You look troubled. That's what I see. Frowns make wrinkles and pull a face down so it looks drawn and thinner.'' She puckered her lips and sucked in her cheeks to demonstrate.

Ariel laughed softly. "I'll smile, then all my wrinkles will curve upward.''

Virginia squeezed her hand. "You always were such an obedient child.''

"Mother, it's not nice to lie.''

"Mothers are blind to children's faults. You'll learn that when you have some.'' Virginia narrowed her eyes slightly. "Why are you troubled?''

"I'm less so now. I wanted to tell you about Siske but—''

"Ariel, it's always been your way to tell me a problem in your own good time. Remember when my favorite lamp got broken? You glued it together, thinking I wouldn't notice. It took you three days before you told me about it.''

"I didn't break it.''

"I knew that. That tall, lanky boy who ducked his head at every doorway broke it while twirling the basketball on his finger. He was always doing that. I often wondered if he went anywhere without his basketball.''

"Nowhere,'' Ariel informed her. "You never told me before that you knew.''

Virginia hunched forward and caressed her cheek. "You have a good heart, but sometimes you can get hurt because of it. And knowing that your father didn't like him, I didn't say anything because I didn't want to see you hurt.''

Ariel leaned forward and hugged her. The sound of a door slamming pulled them apart and turned their attention toward the kitchen doorway.

"Ariel, you're here already." Evan strolled into the room, cradling a bag. "Did you settle that matter with the police?"

The doorbell buzzed once, quickly.

"That's Peter," Evan announced. "No one else rings the doorbell in quite that way."

While Ariel reiterated the story about the police to Evan, her mother let Pete in.

Evan set champagne glasses before the four of them. Conversation jumped from Virginia's play to Ariel's problem with Siske, then to Pete's concern about Carol Jamison, before Evan cleared his throat as if preparing to make an announcement.

"Ginnie and I have made a decision we'd like to share with both of you."

Ariel met Pete's gaze. He looked worried. She wished he didn't. Though Ariel might have difficulty with all the rules in Evan's controlled life, her mother would know best what was right for herself.

"Ginnie is going to move in with me," Evan announced.

Pete's head reared back. "Move in?"

"Not marry?" Ariel asked.

Evan held Virginia's hand. "No, we decided not to get married. Not yet."

"We've only known each other a few months," Virginia reminded them. "We don't think we should rush into marriage."

"And I suggested," Evan added, "that we live together."

Pete hunched forward, concerned. "Dad, what about the college?" He hesitated, searching for words. "Certain people won't approve. What about your chance to get that appointment? You could get that position, but—"

Evan raised a hand to stop him. "I don't want it."

"What?"

"I don't want it, Peter. It will take up a great deal of my time. Time," he said, looking at Virginia, "that I don't want to give up. Once before, I was too busy and too involved. It cost me a great deal." He squeezed Virginia's hand. "Not this time," he said simply.

Ariel saw her mother's worry over Pete's reluctance and pushed back her chair to walk around the table. "I'm happy for you. For both of you," she said, hugging her mother and then Evan.

Pete went through the motions. He smiled, he hugged, he offered good wishes, but Ariel sensed his wariness. His sensitivity would guide him to accept their parents' news eventually. For her mother's sake, Ariel hoped he wouldn't take too long.

Chapter Ten

"Are you surprised?" Ariel asked.

Pete negotiated the car into traffic. "Shocked. Do I drive you toward home or the store?"

"The store. I closed early for this unexpected celebration. Rosie isn't working tonight," she added, wondering if any of the store owners would come to the meeting.

"Is Rosie the elf with the round face who's always got her nose stuck in a book?"

"That's Rosie. At thirty-one and divorced, she's decided that she's made several mistakes in her life. She married too young, she lacks the education to build a career, and she wants to see the world. So she announced one day she'd return to school, make more money, and then she could travel more."

"Sensible."

Ariel laughed. "If you knew Rosie well, you wouldn't say that. At fifteen she married a man twice her age, and divorced him two years later. After that she joined a religious cult in Death Valley, drove a truck for two years, and got a brown belt in karate."

"Interesting."

"Yes, she is."

"Your kind of person."

Ariel shifted to look at him. "I used to believe people needed a great deal in common to be close. But—but look at our parents. They're not alike at all."

"No, they're not." Pete wheeled the car into a fast-food restaurant.

"What are you doing?"

"You haven't eaten yet, have you?"

Ariel wagged her head.

"Then we'll get something and take it back to your store with us."

She gave him a steady look. Us, she thought, clinging to the term he'd used.

He stopped the car in the take-out line and responded to the brightly colored plastic clown requesting his order.

"Eight tacos?" Ariel repeated with incredulity.

"They were two for a dollar. How could anyone resist that kind of bargain?"

"Well, I hope you're hungry, because you're going to eat six of them."

"If we have any left, we'll eat them for breakfast," he declared as he inched the car up to the window.

She noted the mischievous grin tugging the corners of his lips upward. It was a look he was stingy with, a look that revealed a boyish spirit lurking beneath his seriousness.

"It'll probably take us all night to discuss our parents," he remarked.

"Is that what you planned?"

He heard an invitation in her voice.

"Talking?" she asked.

He shrugged. "What else?"

Ariel said nothing, waiting until he glanced her way again. "I'll think of something. I'm very inventive."

His laugh drifted over her—warm, intimate, and full of devilment. "If you don't, I will."

"We can eat them back there," Ariel informed him as she preceded him down the aisle of glassware toward the back of her store.

Pete stood in the center of the storeroom. Though clean, it was cluttered. He skimmed the stacked crates and boxes. "Where?" He directed the question to her back as she wound a path around the boxes and headed toward the front of the store again.

"It's your turn to be inventive," she called back.

Pete eyed several crates, then shoved two closer to a larger one.

Ariel strolled back, a cloth in her hand. "I opened the shop. If someone comes in, we'll hear the bell above the door." She fanned out a multicolored tablecloth and draped it over the largest crate.

Pleased with his handiwork, Pete gestured toward the makeshift table. "I found two crates that are approximately nine inches shorter than the large one."

"Did you measure them?"

"No, I have a pretty good eye for . . ."

Ariel giggled at his serious, businesslike tone.

Pete grimaced. "You would have grabbed the two closest crates."

"That would have made sense to me." She set two brightly colored ironstone candle holders on top of the cloth.

As she pushed red candles into the holders, Pete dug into his pants' pocket for matches. "I'm still amazed," he said, sitting down on one of the crates and lighting the candles.

Ariel peeked into the bag before retrieving two of the paper-wrapped tacos.

"My father." Pete laughed and shoved straws into the plastic lids of cups. "I never thought he'd do anything but marry her. *He* suggested that they live together."

"What about my mother? *She's* the one who doesn't want to rush into anything. My mother's middle name is impulsive." Ariel handed him a napkin. "She might be more of a ponderer than I ever realized."

"And he might be more of a romantic."

Ariel smiled. "Because he gave her that balloon?"

"Among other things," he said, watching her tongue swipe at her top lip to capture a dab of the spicy sauce. He decided that she was deliberately trying to drive him mad.

"Maybe it is love," she said. "He did something unnatural for him, but he did it because he knew she'd be pleased." She chewed slowly, studying his eyes. At times they darkened with a look that made her limbs feel soft.

"I understand that," he said, studying her. A hint of puzzlement knitted her brows. "There isn't any other woman I'd spend twelve hours at the movies with but you."

His admission made her feel pleasurably warm.

As Pete wiped his hands with the napkin, he considered his father again. All he wanted for Evan was happiness.

Seeing the flicker of concern creep back over his face, Ariel touched his hand assuringly. "Pete, they'll be okay. My mother won't hurt him."

He smiled wryly, amazed that she'd guessed his thoughts. "I'd like to believe that. I'm sure my mother never planned to fall in love with another man or cause so much anguish. She tried to explain that to me."

Ariel hunched forward. Through all the time they'd spent together, he'd always avoided talking about his mother. That he'd begun to share that painful time in his life with her meant a great deal. "How old were you?"

"Fifteen. Old enough to understand passion." He shrugged. "But—but I still couldn't forget how I'd felt that morning when I found him sitting at the kitchen table, holding a note and crying."

As his sadness was revealed to her, her heart ached for his pain.

"He was like a different man after that." His eyes clouded. "For nearly two years he barely functioned. At first, after she left and the shock lessened, he took off to find her. He seemed frantic to see her again, talk to her. I suppose he tried to convince her to come back." He finished chewing with difficulty, his mouth suddenly dry. "I didn't care by then. She'd taken our world and left us empty. And—" he paused and dropped the taco on a napkin "—I knew I'd be all right, but I was so damned scared he wouldn't be. And he was all I had."

He looked up, his eyes were blank. She knew he wasn't seeing her. Caught up in the memory, he sat so still that she was frightened for him. She wanted to wrap her arms around him, protect and comfort him.

"He acted crazy for a while. And then there was an accident. The media snapped at it. They dug up all the details about why the professor's wife was five hundred miles from her husband. It was a small-town scandal. It was a nightmare. When he finally came to terms with her being gone and snapped out of it, we moved and he started over.'' His eyes met hers. "Ariel, I don't want to ever see him bleed like that again.''

"You know my mother. She'd never hurt anyone.''

He smiled weakly. "There are some similarities. Like Virginia, my mother was beautiful and charming and eager to experience everything.''

"But your father admitted something this evening. He said that he wouldn't make the same mistake, Pete. I think he realized that he took your mother for granted.'' She slid her hand over his. "He isn't going to make that same mistake with my mother. And Pete, they—they both are compromising.''

"Is that enough?''

"Why don't you think it is?'' she asked, strugging not to let her frustration edge her voice with sharpness.

"Are you sure that she isn't in an I'm-in-love-with-a-professor phase?''

"Phase?''

"Ariel, when you and I were dating before, I saw Virginia go through a ceramic phase, a hospital-volunteer phase, and an aspiring-actress phase.''

"She still makes ceramics and works at the hospital. And acting isn't a phase.''

His brows pulled together. "It isn't?''

"My mother was an actress. She performed in several community theater plays.''

"Your mother did?''

"Yes. She loves to act.'' Ariel's voice softened with affection. "All the time,'' she admitted.

Her honest observation amazed him. "You're aware that she's always on stage?''

"Not always. But most of the time. You should see her when the electric bill arrives. Bette Davis would die of envy over her performance."

"And my father? Who is he seeing?"

His doubting tone irked her. Ariel stifled her temper, aware of the deep-rooted hurt that aroused such skepticism in Pete. "Your father is getting a blend of Goldie Hawn, Cybil Sheppard, and Donna Reed."

"And what happens when the performance ends?"

"It never will, Pete. She made my father happy for twenty years because beneath all those alter egos is a strong woman who kept a smile on her face during all the painful months of my father's chemotherapy. He had a woman who made him smile and laugh during the most difficult time in his life. And if life ever gets tough for your father, she'll make it easier for him, too."

Her words forced him to draw a long breath. "I never knew that about your dad."

"It was a difficult time in our lives." With effort, she kept her voice steady. "He'd always talked of seeing so many things, and I felt so bad, because time had run out for him."

"So you wanted to see the world for him?"

"I thought I did."

"Ariel, that's all you talked about. You wanted to travel, didn't you?"

"I'm not sure I did. I know I wished that he'd had more time to." She met his gaze. "I might have liked to see New York, though."

Something slammed hard against his chest. "Are you telling me that you wanted to go with me?" She said nothing. Her eyes gave him her answer. An ache constricted his throat as he considered the wasted years. "Why didn't you say something?"

She held his gaze despite a cowardly shiver that urged her to retreat. "You never asked me," she said unevenly.

Stunned, Pete looked away. The moment, filled with painful honesty, left him breathless. He sucked in air, feeling too many emotions pulling at him. All the control he prided himself on possessing nearly crumbled. He pushed away everything but the love he felt for her now and before, the love that he'd never really allowed to flow freely through him. All he wanted now was never to make a mistake again. Never to hurt her again.

The sound of the store's bell yanked him from his ponderings. He looked up to see Ariel shoot a look toward the cash-register counter, her eyes widening.

When she dashed from the storeroom, Pete jerked to a stand and rushed after her, ready to charge in front of her if she was in danger. His imagination was working overtime, he decided instantly as he stared at the slim, slightly frightened face of a young Mexican man.

Ariel stood inches from him, holding his hands in hers. "Oh, Carlos, I'm so glad you came."

"Only me." His dark eyes darted to Pete and he pulled back, cringing in the manner of a small, trapped animal.

"You can talk in front of him," Ariel assured Carlos quickly. "He's a friend."

Pete winced. They were more than friends. His look went unnoticed as she stepped closer to Carlos again.

"My father refused to come. He is stubborn," the young man said in a disgusted tone, and stretched to look toward the storeroom.

"No one else came," Ariel informed him. "They must not have thought my idea of a meeting was very good."

"What meeting?" Pete asked, walking around the cash register counter.

Ariel looked up at him. "I suggested that all of the store owners on our block meet to discuss banding together against Siske."

"I did not think the others would come tonight," Carlos said. "They are even more frightened now."

Ariel tensed. "Something else has happened?"

"You have not heard?"

"Heard what?"

"Mr. Calhoun is in the hospital."

"Who's Calhoun?" Pete asked.

"An artist." Ariel merely glanced at him, her attention drawn to the fright she saw in Carlos's eyes. "What happened to him?"

"He was attacked earlier today. Someone hit him on the head."

"In his gallery?"

"Yes, in his gallery."

"How badly is he hurt?"

"He will be all right. But he has a big goose egg," he added, cupping his large palm to his head to indicate an enormous knob. "The police came and we all said nothing."

Ariel held a steady gaze on his eyes. "Did Mr. Calhoun?"

"He said that he did not see the man."

Ariel nodded. She was going to have to fight Siske alone. "I'll visit him tomorrow."

"My father went to see him at the hospital. Mr. Calhoun will be there only for the night."

Ariel was relieved. If Calhoun was being kept in the hospital only overnight, then his injuries weren't severe. "All right."

"I am going to leave now." Carlos's voice carried an apology to match his expression.

"I understand," Ariel said softly.

"Well, I sure as hell don't," Pete bellowed. "None of you want to get involved. Is that it?"

Ariel urged Carlos toward the door, set out the Closed sign, and locked up before responding to Pete's outburst. "They're scared, Pete."

"You aren't? Are you Superwoman suddenly?"

Sensing an ensuing argument from him, she whirled away and headed back toward the storeroom. Quickly she grabbed a crowbar and began opening a crate.

"Are you listening to me?" Pete said.

"I'm hearing you."

He released a harsh oath. "What are you doing now?"

"Opening a crate."

"Why?"

"To keep busy."

"Why?"

"Because if you keep yelling and my hands aren't busy, I might slug you."

"Give me that," he said, stepping close and gently shoving her aside with his hip. "You told me the police are involved."

"They are. And I told my mother about Siske this evening, but she already knew. It seems she heard about him from Mrs. Tremble weeks ago. And as I feared, she was preparing to do battle."

"That doesn't surprise me. She's your mother. But let's take a step back."

She watched him fiercely yank at the metal clips that clamped the top of the crate. More fiercely than necessary, she thought.

"Finish telling me what the police are going to do," he said.

"I talked to Detective Hernandez. You remember him?"

Pete made a face. "How could I forget him?"

She touched his shoulder in passing and then began opening a smaller crate. "I'm glad your sense of humor is still lurking near."

"Forget my humor," he said in a less angry tone. "What did Hernandez say?"

"He believes Siske has been giving me time to consider the possibility of how easily someone, namely him, could break into my store and ruin everything."

"Everything could include your head from what we just heard."

"That's a possibility." She looked back at him. Her eyes flew wide as she realized he'd taken over prying off the lid of a crate that she hadn't meant to open. "Don't..."

Flipping up the final clip, Pete jerked his head around to look at her. "What?"

The warning came too late.

Blue plastic ballooned out of the crate and sprang up from it like a monster. As it floated down between them, Pete's gaze followed its descent. "What the hell—"

"Now you've done it." Staring down, Ariel inched a path around the raft. "It's one of those kind that you can carry with you anywhere," she said, reaching into the crate. "See?" she added, holding a pouch slightly larger than her hand. "Deflated, the raft is folded and packed in one of these. That one," she said, jabbing a finger toward the floor, "is for display. Only I wasn't going to display it just yet."

"You're going to display this?"

"It's one of my best sellers every fall."

"Who buys it?"

"College students."

"The closest river is . . ."

An impish smile curved the edges of her lips. "They don't use them on the water."

His head turned slowly in her direction. "Where do they use them?"

Ariel nudged him in passing, choosing lighthearted play to calm and sidetrack him from their discussion about Siske. "Figure that out for yourself."

She'd taken only one step away when his hand snaked out around her waist. As he fell back onto the raft, he pulled her down with him.

"We've only opened one crate." Ariel squirmed beneath his lips.

"Do you want to unpack more?"

She stared down at him, considering the question for a moment. "You have something else planned?"

He hesitated a second, aware of what she was doing. Having already made a decision to keep a closer eye on her, he saw no reason not to enjoy the less serious moment. He flipped over, pinning her beneath him. "Guess," he answered, popping the button on her jeans.

A teasing grin curled her lips and a giggle flowed up from her throat. "Not too subtle."

Tugging at her jeans and pulling them down, he muttered on a struggling breath, "A little cooperation wouldn't hurt."

Ariel released a low, husky laugh as she raised her hips.

"That's your best effort?" he asked on a soft chuckle, using his foot to push the tight denim off one of her legs.

Ariel curled an arm around his back and turned her face upward. "I could do better."

When her teeth fastened on his earlobe and the warmth of her breath fanned his ear, he felt desperation mingling with his humorous mood. "Would you, please?"

Ariel laughed. "Certainly." She wedged her hand between them. As her fingers slithered beneath his shirt, tugging it from his pants and slowly tracing down the rock hardness of his stomach, she heard his sharp gasp. With her other hand she eased down the zipper. Its raspy sound was overshadowed by his soft groan. She stared into eyes that were bright with passion. "Better?" she asked softly, closing her hand over him.

His mouth captured hers, ending the teasing play. Her taste clouded his mind. He had but one thought—pleasure her. Pleasure her until the emotion pounding through him swept over her. "You make me senseless," he murmured, burying his face into the curve of her neck.

Ariel smiled against his cheek. No more words were needed.

The next morning Pete made a trip to the police station. After getting answers to several questions about Siske, he decided to glue himself to Ariel's side during the next few days.

On Saturday, sunlight glaring against the window of his car, he zipped it into the crowded parking lot of Albuquerque's Old Town.

"I'll be your official tour guide," Ariel insisted.

Without looking at her, Pete knew she was smiling. He could hear happiness in her voice. While living in New York, he used to dream of her, see her smile, hear her voice. Whenever he had, her voice had sung with the same bright, bubbly tone he heard now.

"You'll enjoy yourself," Ariel rambled on as they strolled through the parking lot.

Pete balked slightly, forcing her to slow her exuberant stride. "You're going to owe me a night at one of those thoroughly depressing movies."

She sighed exaggeratedly, holding down a smile. The teasing was a part of him few people saw. She enjoyed the glimpses of his less serious side too much not to play along with him. She kept her hand, unrelenting, on his. "A deal. Now, come on," she coaxed him. "I bet you don't know any of the history."

"What's to know? There's a bunch of old buildings. People use them as stores now."

"See how unappreciative you are of famous landmarks?"

"I've seen famous landmarks," he said, but he docilely moved along with her.

The sun was bright and the air was warm, filled with the faint sounds of strumming guitars. He'd been teasingly complaining since she'd suggested spending their day strolling the cobblestone streets, but he was exactly where he wanted to be on a Saturday morning. He watched sunlight dance off her hair. For years a memory of its scent had overshadowed every other woman's fragrance.

"First, it's imperative that you look like a tourist." She took a step back and squinted at him seriously.

"I'm not one."

"Pete, are you going to cooperate?"

"It depends."

She moved close to him and dropped her head onto his shoulder. "Are you?"

Laughter welled up within him as she batted her eyelashes. "You're crazy."

"Behind that impenetrable stony look lurks a daredevil, doesn't it?" she teased, noting amusement in his eyes. As she ran a fingertip down his cheek, he felt love's force and the sense of contentment that only love could stir.

"I love the way the crease in your cheek deepens when you're trying to look stern," she said.

"What do I have to do to fit your image of a tourist?"

"Let's see." She whirled in place and scanned store windows. "A-ha."

"A-ha, what?"

"Come on," she urged, grabbing his hand and leading him across the cobblestone street and into a store.

Pete grimaced when she set a huge sombrero on his head.

Ariel inclined her head and stared speculatively up at him. "Dashing."

"Foolish."

A corner of her lips curled. "Makes my heart flutter," she said, tapping her chest.

He raised a hand and pushed the wide brim back, then slipped an arm around her waist and caught her to him. *"Señorita."*

Ariel giggled, having anticipated his attempt to say something romantic in Spanish. "Wasn't Spanish the only subject you didn't get an A in?"

"Boy, are you good at killing a mood."

She squirmed from him and danced away. "Wasn't it?"

"More memorable," he said, dropping the hat onto the store counter. He trailed her outside, enjoying the view of her swaying hips. "It was the only one that I flunked."

Ariel flashed a smile back at him. "What did you get in history?"

"What I always got."

She rolled her eyes upward. "Brain man," she mumbled. "Well, I'm going to further your education." She swept her arm toward the center of the plaza. "We begin with the original San Felipe deNeri church. The church was the only real structure here until 1790." Ariel faced the adobe building, which had Gothic features and twin spires. "Between 1610 and 1640, ranches were started in this area." She shifted from one foot to the other and pointed to another building. "That was a grocer's store in 1891."

Pete gave the hipped-roof structure his best interested look, but when she shot a quick grin at him, he felt a shaft of longing cut through him. It was more than passion. He wanted her to be his. He wanted the certainty that they'd know more of those special quiet moments, more of those maddening passionate ones, more of the exciting happy ones they'd always shared. With that longing, he felt fear skitter through him that what he wanted most in life he might not ever get. The thought was too dismal to consider for very long.

Ariel took several steps forward. "That building originally housed a saloon and a barber shop, and the two-story brick near it with the Queen Anne style and the bay windows once belonged to a merchant." She looked back to see if Pete was still following. "What are you doing?"

"Sitting," he said, plopping down on a bench.

"We haven't even started walking yet and you're tired?"

"How much more are you going to tell me?"

"I was done."

He raised himself from the wrought-iron bench.

Ariel planted her feet and laid a fist on her hip. "Are you insinuating that I'm long-winded?"

"On occasion." He couldn't help smiling. "Is that your angry look?"

Ariel sighed exaggeratedly. "Obviously it isn't having any effect on you."

He caught up with her and pulled her hip against his. "But everything else you do does."

"That got you off the hook."

Pete laughed. "What did you do? Memorize the tour guide?"

"Didn't your father ever tell you about any of this?"

"Not this history." Pete's lips curved as a memory flashed back at him. "But during dinner he used to discuss the major political events that occurred in England around 1140. Or he'd expound on the years of Henry the Eighth's reign, especially his marriage to Catherine of Aragon."

"Did you discuss a few beheadings?"

He grinned. "Only famous ones."

"I hope Evan doesn't plan on such dinner conversation with my mother."

"I doubt she'd let him," he said lightly.

"True. Mother would hum her way through the meal so she didn't have to listen to him."

"No, you're the one who hums when faced with something unpleasant. Do you still?"

"Never," she lied, and pulled an arm's length from him to peer up close to one of the bricks. "I wonder what the masons used to build castles. Do you know?"

As she whipped her head over her shoulder to look at him, Pete pointed a finger at his chest. "You're asking me? Mr. Handyman? You fixed the broken toaster, not me."

"That's right. I did. And the dishwasher," she added pridefully. "And—"

"I was good at grocery shopping." His brows bunched. "Wasn't I?"

"Superb," she assured him, whirling back to him and kissing his cheek.

He tightened his grip on her waist again. "You could use someone to do it for you again. A mouse would starve on what you keep in your cupboards."

Ariel turned her face from him and stared at one of the many flat-roofed adobe buildings. "Adobe bricks are formed of mud and straw and then sun-baked. The architecture is fascinating, with its *vigas* and *latillas*."

He tugged her closer, insisting on her attention.

"It's not so simple," she said.

"Do you expect me to hurt you again?"

"Not intentionally."

He stared long at her. Was she unwilling to forgive him for what he'd done before, or was she afraid to? How could he make her understand that he'd died a little every day without her? "Answer one question. Do you really love me?"

She took a long breath. "I love you."

Pete softened the pressure of his arm on her back and then laced his fingers through hers. Tension no longer made him feel as if he were strangling. Words of love came easy during passion, but she'd admitted her feelings for him here, under the sunlight, in the middle of the day, with families of tourists milling around them. He knew now that he wouldn't let her out of his life. Not ever. "Let's walk down there," he said, pointing.

"That street?"

"That's not a street. It's a brick path. And what in the devil are '*vigas*' and '*latillas*'?"

"*Vigas* are the wooden beams that support the roof. *Latillas* are stripped branches layered between the *vigas*."

"Interesting."

"Liar." She laughed before crossing the street in the direction of a lemonade stand. "I'm thirsty." Her voice trailed off as she looked back. He'd disappeared. She cast a glance around her, searching for him. He couldn't have vanished that quickly, she decided, then caught a glimpse of his dark head inside a toy store. Ariel frowned. Why in the world would he go in there?

Pete reappeared, clutching a stuffed animal. Lavender with yellow polka dots, the dragon had a silly grin.

"For you," he said.

Ariel accepted it like an eager child, then held it at arm's length and eyed it speculatively. "It needs a name."

"Give it one so you won't have to wonder if it's a he or a she."

Ariel closed the distance between them and coiled her arms around his neck. "Why did you buy this?"

"Your knight looked lonely." He brushed a knuckle across her cheek. "And everyone needs someone."

Darkness shadowed the cobblestone streets when they left for his apartment.

Ariel whirled in place, absorbing the crisp, sophisticated atmosphere of his black-and-white living room. "Why did we come to your apartment?" she called out as she strolled toward the kitchen.

"I have more in my cupboards than sugared alphabet cereal and peanut butter cookies." Standing at the stove, he glanced back at her. He saw her frowning as she paused in the arched doorway between the rooms. "You don't like it?" he asked.

Ariel swiveled her head around and again scanned the immaculate living room, with its massive bookcase and ebony coffee table, then wandered toward him. With two fingers she cautiously picked a fried potato from the pan. Her stomach rolled in appreciation of the perfect blend of onion and pepper mixed with the potatoes. Eager for more, she looked to her right to grab a fork from the opened silverware drawer. Knives, forks, and spoons were in designated slots. The pots in his kitchen were lined up by size in a cabinet beneath the sparkling-clean stove. "Pete, you're disgustingly organized. I bet you still roll your socks, don't you?" she asked, watching him dredge pork chops in bread crumbs.

"All but the cotton ones."

"Is there a dried-out pen in your apartment?"

"Why would you want a dried-out pen?"

"As a symbolic memento."

"Of what?"

"Something that isn't where it should be."

He chuckled. "If it's dried out, I probably tossed it in the garbage."

"So even that pen found its proper place. I don't remember you ever being quite this neat before."

His lips curved in a quick grin. "If I messed it up, would you stay?"

"Stay?"

"Permanently."

Ariel smiled and strolled around the breakfast bar. "Wouldn't people have a gay old time with that piece of gossip." Settled on one of the bar stools, she reached across the counter for a brown leather binder that was propped against the wall. As she flipped back the cover, she couldn't run from the love they'd once shared. She stared down at the photographs from one of their camping trips—silly ones of her trying to hook a worm or him standing in shorts and a T-shirt and grimacing while starting a fire in the rain. Lovingly, she ran her fingers across a photo of him sitting with a sleeping bag draped around his shoulders as he watched the sunset.

"I thought you'd like to look at them again," he said.

She met his gaze. "We had fun."

His voice softened. "We did." He dropped the pork chops into the frying pan and then dried his hands on a towel. "Stay," he said again.

"What about the gossip?"

He leaned across the counter, bringing his face close to hers. "What gossip?"

"My mother moves in with your father. Then we—"

"Get married. I'm not asking you to move in with me this time." He searched her face. "I'm asking you to marry me."

Ariel released a shaky breath. "I've been married, Pete."

"What does that mean? You only get one chance and you blew it?"

"No, I don't think that." Ariel rushed from the stool and stared out the window. She watched a small boy on a tricycle. His dark hair fluttered beneath the breeze as he pedaled fast, racing his bike down the sidewalk. "I'd never be a model wife."

"You'd be great with our children," he said, standing close behind her.

"Pete, I tried marriage. I never did anything right. Jonathan wanted what you need. Someone who'll set a beautiful table and all those other things." She closed her eyes as his breath warmed the side of her neck and his arm slid across her stomach like a firm band.

"You set a beautiful crate."

Ariel leaned back and relaxed against him. She felt him smile against her cheek. "You'd need someone who'd be able to provide more for her guests than peanut butter cookies."

"So you don't cook. I'm not marrying a cook."

"I like clutter. You're neat."

"I'm willing to appreciate clutter."

She laughed softly. "Pete, it's too soon."

"Not for me. I love you. I love you even more now than I did before. I know now what I gave up." He turned her in his arms. "I'm not giving you up again."

She brushed her hand over his cheek. She wanted to say everything he wanted to hear, but the memory of a previous pain still lingered, stirring her doubts. "I love you."

Gently he kissed her palm.

"For now," Ariel whispered, "please don't ask for more."

Hurt entered his eyes. "Why?"

"I can't give more." *I'm too afraid,* she thought. *I'm too afraid I'll believe in us again, and you'll walk away like you did before.* She kept the thought to herself as he drew her close. She clung to him, wishing they'd transcended the doubts she had about their future, wishing all of that was behind them.

Chapter Eleven

A six-letter word for merry," Ariel whispered. "Starts with a j."

Pete shifted on the cushioned seat in the college auditorium and looked up from the program in his hands. "You're addicted."

"Agreed," she returned, and tapped the pencil at the evening newspaper's crossword puzzle. "Help me. The play will begin in a few minutes and I won't have this done."

"Bliss." It was the emotion he'd felt through the past week.

"Only five letters. And it starts with a j," she repeated.

She concentrated on the newspaper; he studied her. The overhead lights slanted across the top of her head, paling the vibrant hue of her hair. Against the rich royal blue of her silk dress, her skin looked like porcelain. He watched the slight flutter of her thick lashes. They cast a faint shadow on her face. Sometimes his head swam just from looking at her.

"Well?" Her deep blue eyes, which reminded him of the sea beneath bright sunlight, suddenly met his. "Do you know?"

Pete rolled the program in his hand. "I know that you're beautiful."

She watched his gaze sweep over her face in a slow, memorizing manner. Silk rustled beneath her as she angled her body toward him. "You're beautiful, too," she said in an amused tone.

"Jeez." Pete turned his face away.

"You are," she insisted in a soft, teasing voice as the lights dimmed and a hushed quietness floated across the large room.

As he looked back at her, she bent her head close to his. His breath fluttered across her face. She hadn't lied—there was a beauty to his face. When he looked cool and businesslike, a tenseness sharpened the angles and hardened his features. In softer moments, like now, the classic lines of his face would have tempted the great sculptors.

The time she'd spent with him lately had pulled them closer. Somehow the headiness of love had blotted out her previous objections. Since his return she'd been following an alien path while she tried to foresee the future. "I've been thinking," she said suddenly.

Pete smiled, because she looked so serious. "You have? About what?"

"Marriage."

Despite the darkness surrounding them, he could see the sparkle in her eyes.

"And babies. Do you like babies?"

He let out a long breath, unable to take his gaze off her lips. "I have no idea."

"Make a guess," she requested.

He raised his eyes to hers. He saw expectation. Anticipation. Emotion swamped him. "I'd say yes."

"Funny," she whispered, bringing her face inches from his, "but I never really cared if any other man did."

He was silent for the moment. He acknowledged the sound of voices drifting from the stage but heard none of the words.

"Still want to get married?" she asked, smiling. "Because if you do, I do."

He felt as if she'd stopped the world for this moment. Her gaze never wavered from his. He saw no tease, no uncertainty. Joy spiraled through him, and he released a quick, soft laugh that turned heads toward him. He didn't care. Nothing mattered but her. Heat rose in his body, the need to pull her to him curling around him with the force of a whirling tornado. "You picked the damnedest place to tell me that," he said with incredulity.

Her lips quickly met his. "I'll repeat that later," she whispered, settling back on her seat but slanting a quick, promising glance at him.

He sat back, too, and attempted to concentrate on the play, but he wished it were over instead of only beginning. He wanted her alone. He listened to the voices coming from the stage, but her voice as she'd said those words lingered in his mind. He caught little of the performance beyond joining in a laughing moment or noting the professional edge of Virginia's acting. Blind with emotion, he sat through the play in a foggy existence, snapping back to the reality of his surroundings only when the clamor of applause and the brightening of the auditorium's lights forced him to.

As he stood with Ariel to leave, his hand found hers. The quick, firm clasp symbolized the tight hold she had on his heart, the tight hold she would always have.

She preceded him up the aisle, then waited, stalled at the exit by the confusion of others. Standing among the crowd, she felt as if they were alone. She stared back at him, saw in his eyes the reflection of the love she felt for him, and the moment seemed to belong only to them.

She noted that his hand never left her. It clasped with hers or touched the small of her back or caressed the nape of her neck. He needed the same nearness, the same intimacy, she did, she realized as they stepped outside. She hesitated before reminding him, "We're invited to the cast party."

"To celebrate?" Pete asked as they filed away from the theater entrance along with the others who'd just witnessed an unusual version of *The Taming of the Shrew*.

Ariel nudged him with an elbow. "The play was a success."

"That's debatable. But I'd say that your mother was. I'm not too sure how a critic would view the other players."

"She was good, wasn't she?" Ariel said pridefully. "And she covered up several mistakes so well that I'm sure the audience never guessed."

"Like rushing forward when Lucentio tripped over the cardboard step?"

Ariel looked up at him. Her eyes danced as moonlight washed the deep color from them and emphasized their sparkle. "She did do a marvelous job of feigning concern as Bianca. And only a few times did the audience guess that she was shyly turning her face from them to cue Baptista.''

Pete slipped an arm around her waist and urged her toward his car. "I suppose we should go to the party and help her celebrate.''

Thoughtfully, Ariel stared up at him. His willingness to share in her mother's happiness meant a great deal to her. "You're not displeased anymore about our parents living together?'' Ariel asked hopefully. At his shrug, she went on. "It might be a good idea.''

"No,'' he answered simply.

Her smile faded.

"I give them three months, tops.''

Ariel stared down at her feet. Their parents deserved happiness. She knew her mother well. If Virginia felt Pete's reluctance to accept her, she'd be concerned about placing a wedge between him and his father. "I wish—''

"I know what you wish.''

They stood on the curb. As an impatient driver blasted his horn at a late-night bus, Pete cupped a hand on Ariel's arm to keep her beside him.

"I give them three months until they get married,'' Pete finished.

Her lips curved upward instantly. "I thought...I thought...well...'' She turned and placed a hand on his chest. Beneath her palm his heart hammered a steady, strong beat. "I thought you weren't listening to me before when I tried to explain about her.''

"I listened. I'd say my dad was lucky to find her. Almost as lucky as me.''

"Lucky?''

He laughed at her pleased look. "You're wonderful.''

"Thank you.''

"And wild. And jocund.''

Ariel arched a brow.

"Six-letter word starting with j that means merry."

Ariel laughed and swayed against him.

"What made you finally give the right answer?" he asked.

She pulled her head back to see his face more clearly. A hesitation entered her voice. "You won't laugh if I tell you?"

"I won't."

"Promise."

"I promise."

Ariel bent her head and unclasped her purse.

Pete frowned at the broken piece of a fortune cookie she held between her fingers. Then he laughed.

"You promised you wouldn't do that," she reminded him.

He tightened his arms on her. "What did it say?"

"Marriage is a new beginning."

A gentle breeze whipped around them. As her hair flew forward he raised a hand and brushed it away from her cheek. "About that party..."

She grinned crookedly. "No one will miss us."

For a week Ariel hadn't heard from Siske. She'd started to believe that she'd never see him again, but on Monday morning he began to play on her nerves and remind her how vulnerable she was.

Before eleven, a fire started in the garbage receptacle behind her shop, the electrical power to the store mysteriously failed despite brand-new fuses, and beneath the breeze, the store sign above the doorway broke away from the S hooks and crashed to the cement.

If Ariel was nervous, Siske managed to push Rosie into paranoia. She examined the bent S hooks and paled, knowing this was no accident.

Worry mounting within, Ariel contacted the detective. Hernandez listened, soothed her, then took command.

"Everything will be fine," he assured her. "Come to my office tomorrow. I'll explain our plan then."

It sounded simple enough to Ariel. Still, she was petrified.

The voices of Monday-morning fitness addicts echoed through the health club. From a court near the locker room drifted the steady beat of a basketball being dribbled across the gleaming wood floor.

Pete stood near a locker and slipped his racket into the case.

"Hey, where have you been for the past few weeks?" Bill questioned, his words muffled behind a towel as he emerged from the showers.

"Busy." Pete reached into the locker for his shirt. "Who's been beating you on the court?"

"My brother-in-law." Bill flung the towel to the bench that separated the rows of lockers. "And he didn't beat me. I skunked him."

Pete finished buttoning his shirt, then tugged on a pair of slacks. During their set on the racquetball court he'd caught Bill's questioning look more than once. Head bent, Pete grinned as he buttoned a cuff and sat down on the bench to prepare for the inquisition.

"My brother-in-law is a cop. He told me an interesting story about a guy he thought was a friend of mine. Seems this fellow got hauled into the station. You'll never guess who it was."

Pete's fingers paused on a shirt cuff. "Bet I will."

Bill plopped down on the bench beside him as Pete bent forward to tie his shoes. "He told me the guy's name was Peter Turner. I said, 'Nah, that can't be my good buddy Pete. He doesn't even jaywalk.'"

Pete smirked but said nothing.

"But then Joe, my brother-in-law, said that a woman came down to the station, and this fellow Pete was released. I thought, okay, maybe that is good old Pete. Before a certain redhead came into his life, he was a fast worker, so he could have found a lady to get him out of a jam."

Pete stood and tucked his shirt into his pants.

"*If* that guy was the Pete I knew." Bill slanted a look at him. "But I didn't think so. And then Joe said that the woman was a real looker. A redhead with this odd name."

Pete shrugged into his suit jacket and grinned down at Bill before heading toward the exit.

"Ariel," Bill called out.

Pete paused in midstride and looked back. "Was there ever anyone else?"

"Smart man!"

Pete felt like one. High IQ's meant nothing. He'd made a stupid mistake years ago and had finally corrected it.

The aroma of freshly brewed coffee greeted him as he entered his office. The door clicked behind him, but Muriel's face remained buried behind the sports section.

"Did you win or lose this weekend?" Pete asked.

Muriel mumbled an answer, not looking out from the newspaper.

He made a calculated guess from her unenthusiastic response. "Lost again."

She grunted this time.

He chuckled and strolled into his office. The coffee brewer on a credenza hissed loudly as drops of steaming water hit the warming plate.

After pouring a cup, he settled behind his desk and sorted through the mail that Muriel had set in stacks on his desk. Despite her preoccupation with the race results, she'd already typed yesterday's correspondence. Pete signed the letters, then flipped the cover of a file folder to review a client's previous tax return. An hour later he'd jotted down the first draft of a profile for various ways to invest a portion of the executive's profits and cut his taxes.

Absently Pete curled a finger through the handle of his coffee cup. The cold and bitter-tasting brew coated his tongue. He pushed back his chair to get a fresh cup. Half-standing, he paused and plopped back down to answer Muriel's buzz.

Pete flicked the intercom switch. "So you were alive behind that newspaper?"

"I lost a bundle," she quipped. "J.C.'s on line two."

Her announcement didn't faze him. Everything in his life was going too well. Nothing could go wrong now, he decided, reaching for the receiver.

By the time he finished his conversation and set down the receiver, he felt a little dazed. He leaned back in the chair and drew a long breath, trying to stifle the excitement that urged him to charge from the chair and yell out a cheer. Instead he flicked the intercom switch. "Muriel."

"Coming." Within seconds she appeared at the door. "Something wrong?"

Pete shook his head. "J.C. is coming to town on an afternoon plane."

Deep lines spread out from the corners of her eyes; her broad smile crinkled her face. "Will I have to call you Mr. Turner when you become a senior consultant?"

"Don't jump the gun. I'm not sure he's coming to give me that promotion."

"Sure he is. He's a smart old coot. He knows a good man when he sees him."

Pete ran a hand across his mouth, but he couldn't erase his grin. "I can't sit here. I'm going to take an early lunch. I have to talk to someone."

"Someone?"

"The future Mrs. Turner," he answered, and laughed at her gaping expression.

Ariel wrapped white tissue paper around an Italian crystal decanter and set it in a white gift box. "Thank you," she said, closing the lid and handing it to the woman on the other side of the counter. "And come again."

As the door closed behind the customer, she turned her attention on Rosie. Squatting, she was sweeping a feather duster across several ginger jars on the bottom display shelf. "Rosie, how would you like a few days off?"

Rosie's dark head snapped around. "With pay?"

Ariel nodded. Poor business management, Pete would declare if he knew. But a few dollars lost seemed trivial if it meant keeping Rosie out of danger.

Rosie stood slowly and frowned at her. "Why are you doing this? With college starting soon, we're getting busier."

"You've worked a few days and nights when you weren't scheduled."

Rosie grinned. "Anything for romance. If I had someone who looked like him in my life, I'd want to spend time with him, too. I didn't mind coming in those few times."

"And I appreciated it. Hey," Ariel said, forcing a bright smile, "what is this? Don't you want time off?"

"Yeah." Rosie shrugged. "Sure I do," she admitted, continuing to look concerned. "But—"

"You can get an end-of-the-summer suntan. Or read all those books that you bought."

Rosie dropped the feather duster on a counter. "Ariel, is something wrong? Because if there is..." She paused, then plunged forward. "I could help."

Ariel met her halfway and placed an arm around her shoulder. "I don't have any problems that I can't handle."

"But you do have a problem? I mean—we've had a lot of trouble lately." Lines wrinkled her brow. "A lot. And I don't think that kids are doing all those things."

"Kids start trash fires."

"But you've had things stolen and—"

"Pizza man!" Pete called.

The spicy aromas lured Ariel's attention toward the door as much as his voice did. She inhaled deeply.

"I brought lunch." He winked at Rosie. "I remember you telling me that you hated anchovies, Rosie."

Ariel tilted her head, curious. "When did you two discuss pizza?"

Rosie's complexion darkened. "Oh, a couple of days ago while you were in the back room."

"We decided the best pizza in town had to have everything," he replied. "Except anchovies," he added, smiling at Rosie before passing the enticing carton beneath

Ariel's nose. "And I can't think of anything nicer than lunch with two pretty women."

"I'm leaving," Rosie said, already halfway to the door. "I bought enough."

Rosie grinned at him but kept walking. "Ah, go on." She shimmied a shoulder. "Have an intimate lunch."

"Rosie!" Ariel called out.

But the door had already closed behind her.

Pete laughed.

"She believes everything in the world revolves around romance or sex," Ariel explained.

He leaned across the counter, bringing his face close to hers. "And you?"

Ariel passed her lips across his. Before he could deepen the kiss, she flipped open the carton. "Hmm, that smells great." She lifted a slice out, balancing the tip with the fingers of her other hand. "What brings you over for an unexpected visit?"

"Dinner plans."

Ariel bit into the pizza, nodding.

"J.C. Bryant will be with us."

She swallowed her first bite with difficulty. "Why?"

"Why is he coming?" At her quick nod, he answered, "I hope he's coming to make me Bryant and Bryant's newest senior consultant."

"Oh, Pete. Really?"

"Really." He smiled widely. "I hope. Anyway, he'll be having dinner with us." Some of the pleasure slipped from his face. "Unfortunately so will Carol Jamison."

"The reporter?"

Pete nodded. "She's been in California, writing articles about other firms, but J.C. heard that she was back in Albuquerque this morning. He insisted I invite her to join us."

"It sounds like a business dinner," Ariel said, turning away and reaching under the counter for an opened can of soda.

"It is, but I mentioned you, and J.C. would like to meet you."

"Me?" Ariel spun around and faced him. "Why did you do that?"

"Why shouldn't I?"

"Oh, Pete, what if something goes wrong?"

"What can go wrong? I love you; he'll like you."

"What if I spill catsup on him?"

"Bill doesn't serve catsup at the Hillcrest. His chef would revolt." Her hesitation concerned him. "Don't you want to go?"

"Yes," she answered, but her mind filled with all the possibilities. She could so easily jeopardize what Pete had been working for. She wasn't a klutz, but she recalled all the times she'd gone somewhere with Jonathan. She'd always been on edge, feeling his critical eye on her. And J.C. Bryant symbolized stiff, stuffy, and stodgy.

Pete wanted to reassure her. He saw the tension in her face, felt the hesitation in her acceptance of such an evening. "What happened before between us was my fault. Not yours." He frowned. "I didn't leave you because I was worried that you wouldn't fit in. I wanted you with me."

She whirled around, her eyes widening. "You never said that."

Pete twisted away, the foolishness of his own assumptions haunting him. "You wanted something that I couldn't give." He turned and faced her, holding his palms up in an appealing gesture. "I had no time to traipse around. I was trying to establish a career."

"I knew that."

Pete closed the distance between them. "Yes, but I thought if I'd asked you to marry me, then I'd be asking you to give up something you wanted. I loved you too much to do that."

"I loved you enough to do anything you'd have asked," she said, stepping into his arms.

"Then do this for me. Meet him. I want you to be a part of my life, share it with me."

His eyes were serious and brooding, and they melted her heart. He brushed his thumbs at the edges of her lips as if by touch he could curve them upward. She had never been more aware of her vulnerability, nor of his. "I'll be there," she said softly, and smiled because she knew he wanted to see it, but she had to stifle a nervous flutter in her stomach. "Where and when?" she asked.

"Six-thirty." He kissed the bridge of her nose, wondering how it was possible to love someone so much that the emotion weakened and strengthened him at the same time.

Ariel whirled back to the counter. "Where?"

Pete joined her by the counter again and picked up another slice of pizza. "At the Hillcrest. Do you want me to pick you up?"

An inkling of doubt resurfaced in her. Did he think she wouldn't get there on her own? "No, you'll be busy, won't you?"

"I should pick him up at the airport. But if you want, I could—"

"Pete, the airport is halfway between your office and the Hillcrest. It would be silly for you to drive all this way to get me. I'll be there. Six-thirty," she confirmed, managing a smile even as being burned at the stake appeared less agonizing than meeting J.C. Bryant for dinner.

* * *

"Call me an Indian giver," Ariel said when Rosie returned later, "but I'd like you to stay for a couple of hours. I have a few things to take care of this afternoon. I promise you can have the next few days off."

Rosie leaned back against the counter and eyed the leftover pizza. She picked at some cheese stuck to the round cardboard. "I told you that I didn't care about taking time off."

"No, I insist," Ariel snapped.

Rosie peeked at her.

"I'm sorry." Passing Rosie, Ariel touched her arm. "I'm going next door for a minute to talk to my mother. I'll be right back."

"Okay."

Ariel glanced back. "Want the pizza?"

"I thought you'd never ask."

Virginia was sitting in the middle of the floor in the back room of the floral shop.

Pausing in the doorway, Ariel watched with puzzlement and amusement. "Mother, are you practicing yoga again?"

Virginia's gaze remained on the floor. "No, I lost a swatch. Come down here, dear, and help me search for it."

Ariel complied. On her hands and knees, she peered under the worktable. "What swatch?"

"Oh, I was making bouquets for the Summerfield wedding," she began. "Their daughter is absolutely atrocious," she added. "But Louise Summerfield is such a lovely woman. So when her daughter insisted that the ribbon on her flowers match her dress exactly, I agreed." Virginia crawled in an opposite direction. "Dang this white floor. How can anyone find a white swatch on a white floor?''

Arial sat on her heels. "The swatch is white? What's so difficult about matching a white swatch?''

Briefly, Virginia looked over her shoulder at her. "Not white exactly. Sort of oyster. But not oyster. Maybe..." She sighed heavily. "Well, it's not an ordinary white.'' She inserted her hand between the wall and the back of a storage table. "And as I said, Louise's daughter has not been one of the most pleasant people to deal with. I suppose she's nervous. That would explain her sharp mood, wouldn't it?''

"I suppose," Ariel returned, recalling her snappish response to Rosie. She bent forward, stretching under the worktable. "Here it is.''

"Oh, thank goodness," Virginia said as Ariel handed the sliver of cloth to her. "What color would you call this?''

Ariel shook her head. "I don't know. A yucky yellow-ish white?''

Virginia's hands fluttered in a slicing motion. "Oh, well, never mind.'' She sat up, resting on her knees, and stared at Ariel. "Something is wrong. I can see it in your face. Peter?''

"No, Pete hasn't done anything.''

"Then what is wrong?''

"I'm nervous.''

"You, dear?''

"Pete was just here. Mr. Bryant is coming to town. Pete didn't say it, but I know he was excited. Mother, he's worked hard for a senior consultant's position. I'm sure by the way he acted that he was anticipating good news.''

"How did he act?''

"Not different, but very excited.''

Virginia nodded knowingly.

"I'm sure Pete is hoping that J.C. Bryant is coming here to announce the promotion."

Virginia's eyes brightened. "Wouldn't that be wonderful. Wait until I tell Evan. He'll be so pleased for Pete."

"Yes, but Pete wants me there." Ariel toyed with a strand of her hair. "At the dinner."

"Of course he does. He loves you. And a woman in a man's life, a partner, shows the people who count that the man's responsible and settled down."

Letting the curl of hair slip from her fingers, Ariel tipped her head slightly. Had her mother always possessed such logic and sensibility? "You never concerned yourself with such things before."

"Your father and I led a different type of life." Virginia grabbed the edge of the table and pulled herself to a stand. "He rarely concerned himself with what others thought."

"Yes, and was happier for it."

Puzzled that her mother hadn't responded, Ariel stood beside her and questioned, "Weren't you?"

Virginia turned a smile on Ariel that made her eyes look softer with a warm memory. "Yes, yes, I was happy, but he never really planned for anything. We owned this shop," she said, scanning the room. "But your father often closed it on a whim to go fishing."

Ariel, too, smiled. "Yes, I remember."

"We had some wonderful times, but there were many things that I had to deal with later because he hadn't concerned himself with anything but the moment." An appeal for understanding settled on her face. "But it's different now. I'm getting older, and it's rather nice being with Evan. He gives me a very secure feeling. He thinks ahead, concerns himself about the future. We're even planning next summer's vacation. He wants to see the fjords. I think I'd like that," she said softly. "But you see, he worries what others think about me and him. He doesn't want them to talk badly about me. And that's good, too. I know he does that because he loves me."

Thoughtfully, Ariel stared at her. "I didn't want to go tonight." She released a soft, self-deprecating laugh. "That sounds cowardly, but I made so many mistakes when I was married to Jonathan."

"Did you?"

Ariel met her mother's eyes.

"Did you make mistakes, or did he tell you that?"

"I..." Ariel paused. One of the reasons she'd divorced Jonathan was because he'd belittled her so expertly. After a year of marriage she'd seen him as a sour, cynical man who criticized anything and everything. When had she forgotten that? When had she allowed all the self-doubts to stir again?

As Ariel sighed, Virginia touched her shoulder. "You'll do fine tonight." Her smile widening, Virginia began rummaging through a large carton of ribbons. "Last evening I attended a faculty dinner." Her voice rose in amazement. "And I rather enjoyed it. Everyone was friendly. And the dean's wife even inquired about where I'd bought my caftan. You know, that lovely bright pink and navy one that you gave me for Christmas."

"Yes, I remember," Ariel answered, suddenly aware of why she'd needed to talk to her mother. How simple it would have been for her mother to choose a navy dress and pearls and pretend to be as conservative as the others at the faculty dinner. But that wasn't Virginia Hammond. And though she put her best foot forward, it was *her* foot, not someone else's. "So you had a good time?"

"Wonderful. And the dean's wife invited me to lunch next week. She requested my Polynesian spare ribs recipe. Evan raved about them," she went on brightly. "I haven't told her yet how simple they are to make. But of course, I will." Virginia turned toward her worktable and held a white ribbon beside the swatch. "I doubt I'll ever find a match for this," she said, frowning.

"You'll do a good job."

"Just as you will. You're very clever." Virginia leaned close and whispered as if telling a secret in a room full of people. "We both are."

Ariel reentered the Potpourri Bazaar to find Rosie on the phone. She looked pale. Without saying a word, she handed Ariel the telephone receiver.

Ariel frowned questioningly but took the phone. "Hello."

"I've been talking to your employee."

Ariel tensed, needing no greeting to identify Siske's raspy voice. "You can stop your threats."

He released a quick, harsh laugh. "I thought you'd begin to see things my way. I'll be there at nine-thirty tomorrow evening. Have the money."

"I will." Ariel set the receiver down and met Rosie's frightened look.

"Ariel?"

"Don't worry about it," Ariel assured her, and touched her shoulders, urging her toward the door. "Now, you leave."

Rosie balked, planting her feet. "I can't leave you. What if—"

"Leave now," Ariel insisted, handing Rosie her oversized carryall. "I have to call the police."

Rosie let out a long breath. "Thank goodness. I was afraid you wouldn't. What about tonight?"

"Don't worry about the store." Ariel placed a gentle hand on Rosie's back and strolled with her toward the door. "I'll close the shop."

As soon as Rosie left, Ariel called Detective Hernandez and informed him that Siske had finally arranged a meeting with her.

Throughout the afternoon she glanced at her watch several times. Worried thoughts about handling Siske kept intruding while she tallied the day's receipts, but time was paramount in her mind. She couldn't be late for her dinner meeting with Pete.

At five-thirty she emptied and locked the cash register. She'd allowed herself enough time to go home, change clothes, and arrive at the restaurant at six-thirty.

Grabbing her purse from the floor, she heard the bell above the door. On an uncharacteristic oath, she straightened, wishing she'd locked the door to any more customers.

Emanuel Varquez walked in, followed by a beaming Carlos. One step behind him was Judd Calhoun. The Trembles stood in the doorway.

"We decided you are right," Emanuel said, taking a spokesman's position. "We would like that meeting. It is time we stop that man."

Chapter Twelve

Pete never considered that she wouldn't show up at the restaurant.

At 6:50 he sat at a small round table in the Hillcrest's lounge with J.C. and Carol Jamison.

While J.C. expounded on Bryant and Bryant's merits and accomplishments, Pete's stomach churned and knotted with a wrenching tightness that made him want to reach for the roll of antacids in his pocket.

He looked across the shadowy lounge at the bar. Behind several rows of bottles, the illuminated clock assured him that his watch wasn't running fast. Anxiety gripped him, and he forced himself not to start imagining all the dire incidences that inevitably popped into a person's mind when a loved one was late. She was fine, he told himself once again, but the anxiousness continued to build up pressure in his chest.

Bryant's thick gray brows bunched as he frowned. "Your friend isn't very punctual, Peter."

The thin-faced woman sitting between them tipped her head in a curious manner, her eyes brightening with an eagerness that made Pete tighten his jaw. Beneath her polite facade lurked the journalist who viewed the first amendment as a freedom to ignore the right of privacy if it meant getting "good copy."

"Are you sure the young woman is coming?" J.C.'s displeased tone yanked Pete from his ponderings.

"Who is she?" Carol Jamison questioned.

"Ariel Hammond."

One of her dark brows shot up. "Since the name is such an unusual one, I can't help but recognize it. Isn't she the store owner who had you arrested?"

J.C. noticeably tensed. "Ms. Jamison, I'm sure my people explained the situation to you."

"They offered me a sugar-coated explanation. Mr. Turner dodged all my questions."

"Peter probably thought the matter didn't warrant any further explanation." J.C. glanced around him. "I've been told that this establishment has won several awards for their cuisine. I must say I'm looking forward to sampling the food."

Despite J.C.'s efforts to shift the topic of conversation, the woman kept a steady gaze on Pete. "Pete," she said with an informality that seemed incongruous, "what is the real story? Why were you brought in for questioning? The police don't usually do that unless they're suspicious. Did they have a reason to suspect you of something?" she asked, feigning a laugh as if the idea were ridiculous.

Pete felt the prick of her needle as she tried to draw blood. He looked at the clock again. "I wasn't arrested. The police wanted to ask me a few questions."

"That's right; you weren't. But I don't understand. Why would the police believe such an obvious law-abiding citizen would be involved in any crime?"

Pete gave her a long look, tired of her prodding in an effort to tarnish the firm's image through him and an incident that didn't merit the attention she was giving it. "Ariel Hammond and I are old friends. We returned from dinner and found that someone had tried to break into her shop. After I left her, I was worried, so I returned to her store. The police picked me up then, believing I was the culprit."

"Quite logical," J.C. announced. "A simple mis—"

"Did you invite Ms. Hammond to join us this evening because you thought her appearance would support the story?"

Pete met Carol with a direct look. He didn't like her, and hadn't from the moment she'd stepped into his office. He'd sensed her ambition. If she could liven up an article about the firm by tossing in a little dirt, then she'd stir up controversy. If people talked about the story, wouldn't they also discuss the sharp reporter who'd uncovered any indiscretions? "I invited Ms. Hammond this evening because Mr. Bryant has always indicated an interest in not only his associates but their families."

"I wasn't aware that Ms. Hammond was a relative."

Pete swirled the ice cubes in his drink, fighting a strong urge to smash his glass on the floor. He controlled the anger stirred by her goading. She wanted news—he'd give her news. "She's going to be my wife."

"Peter! Congratulations." J.C. reached across the table and pumped his hand. "That certainly explains why you'd return to her store and be concerned about her. Don't you agree, Ms. Jamison?"

"Yes." She looked confused and annoyed at the unexpected announcement. "It would seem to."

Pete was tired of playing her game and too damn worried about Ariel to sit still another moment. "If you'll excuse me, I'll see if a table is ready for us."

"Aren't we going to wait for your fiancée?" The woman's tone veiled nothing. His explanation hadn't satisfied her, but he couldn't reveal to the press Ariel's involvement in an ongoing investigation of an extortionist.

Quickly he wound his way around tables and inched through the crowd of conventioneers in the restaurant's lobby. Bill Kunutz stood before them. In a soothing tone, the restaurateur attempted to calm the displeased group.

Stopping behind Bill, Pete nudged him to draw his attention away from his frantic-looking maître d'.

"We'll have a table for you in a minute, Pete," Bill responded, not waiting for Pete's question.

As Bill turned a worried frown back at the crowd before him, Pete nudged him again.

Annoyance flashed across Bill's face. "Come on, Pete. I promised you the best table in the place. You'll have it. Give me a minute. Right now I have to handle a foul-up in reservations," he added, glaring at the maître d'.

"Just tell me where there's a damn phone I can use," Pete yelled over the voices of irate conventioneers.

His bellow silenced the crowd.

Slowly, Bill looked back at him. "Uh, yeah, a phone." He frowned, but touched Pete's sleeve. "In my office. Use the one in my office, buddy."

Ariel's shop line was busy.

Pete perched on the edge of the desk. He had to think

logically, sensibly. All his life he'd prided himself on thinking things through clearly, not rushing to conclusions or snap judgments.

If the line was busy, she must still be at the store. Nothing had happened to her, he told himself, listening to the buzz, its sound as annoying as that of a mosquito's drone.

"Trouble?" Bill asked.

Pete whipped around and faced him. "Ariel's late."

Bill lifted his hands in a noncommittal gesture, smiling weakly. "Traffic. She'll be here soon."

Would she be? Pete wondered as he set down the receiver. Doubts blended with troubled thoughts. When he'd asked her to meet Bryant, he'd sensed her reluctance. Had she changed her mind about coming tonight? Had she also changed her mind about marrying him?

Bill clamped a hand on his shoulder. "Pete?"

"Do you have a table for us now?"

"You don't want to wait for her?"

"No." He let out a deep breath, trying to weigh the situation logically, but his emotions guided him. He felt anger, hurt, disappointment. If she couldn't get to the restaurant on time, if she didn't want to meet Bryant, then this evening wasn't important enough to her. He jammed a hand into his pants' pocket, balling his fist. "Something more important to her must have come up."

Bill followed him to the door. "I have a table that overlooks the mountains."

"Thanks. Bryant will be impressed." Pete stepped out of the office and began walking back toward the lounge. He geared himself for the following embarrassing questions about Ariel, Carol Jamison's inevitable snide smile, and Bryant's silent, disapproving look that Pete had chosen such a woman to marry.

The next few moments were going to be hell.

Ariel had spent a half hour calming Mrs. Tremble. "We'll be protected," she said for what seemed the twentieth time.

"How can they protect all of us?" Emanuel Varquez asked.

"The detective I talked to assured me that they would."

"We have to testify, though?" Judd Calhoun questioned.

Ariel glanced at the wide, square bandage on his forehead. "Yes, you all would have to. I'll get the actual evidence, but the district attorney will need all of you to testify in court that Siske threatened you."

Mr. Tremble shook his head and sent his wife a worried look. "I don't know if we should do this."

Carlos shot to a stand. "How can you think that? You—us—we have all been threatened. If you do not do this, you are cowards," he said disdainfully.

His explosive outburst seemed to do him the most good. Ariel scanned the faces of the people seated on crates in the back room of her store. Carlos was adamant; Judd Calhoun was convinced; Emanuel Varquez wavered; the Trembles still trembled; and her mother parroted everything that Ariel had said. Somehow her mother had learned of the meeting and arrived late.

As voices raised and overshadowed one another, Ariel took a long breath. If they didn't stay calm, someone would storm out in a huff and the meeting would be a failure.

She was running out of time. She had to settle them down and get their agreement soon, she thought, glancing at her watch. A giant lump suddenly formed in the center of her stomach. It couldn't be that late. It couldn't be. "Mother, what time do you have?"

Virginia turned her wrist and squinted at the small face of the watch. "Five after seven, dear." Her voice trailed off and her blue eyes widened as they raised to meet Ariel's. "Weren't you supposed to—"

"Damn!" Ariel raced toward the front of the store, ignoring questions behind her.

"What's wrong?"

"Has something happened?"

"Siske! Did she see Siske?"

"He knows we're here, doesn't he?" Mrs. Tremble cried out in a shaky voice.

While Virginia soothed everyone, Ariel slammed the telephone receiver back on its stand. When everyone had arrived, she'd locked the door and placed the receiver on the counter so they wouldn't be disturbed by the phone while they'd had the meeting.

Her throat tightened as she thumbed through the telephone book, looking for the number of the Hillcrest restaurant.

Pete wouldn't forgive her. She'd worried about doing something wrong, and she'd made the supreme faux pas. She'd missed the dinner.

"Bill Kunutz, please," Ariel said quickly. Seconds ticked away with excruciating slowness. Pete still had to be there. Pete and J.C. Bryant and that journalist. Ariel drew a long, hard breath.

"Hello."

"Bill, it's Ariel. Is Pete there?"

"He was in my office trying to get you, but your line was busy."

"Are they eating?"

"They're done with their salads."

Ariel closed her eyes. "Please get him for me."

Tension clenched her stomach. She toyed with the telephone cord, curling it around a finger. Time passed so slowly that she thought it had stopped.

"Ariel?"

"Pete."

"Are you all right?" he asked, concern and relief mingling together now that he heard her voice.

"I'm fine," she said weakly. She heard the anxiousness in his voice. She'd been prepared for anger, that icy, clipped tone he had when he was fighting for control.

"I was worried. You were supposed to be here at six-thirty. Did you have car trouble?"

"No, I didn't."

"You said that you'd be here."

"I know. I'm sorry."

"Where are you?"

"At the store."

Puzzlement edged his voice. "I called the store. The line was busy."

"I took the phone off the hook. Pete, is Mr. Bryant—"

"You took the phone off the hook?" he asked incredulously. "Why would you do that?"

She caught the slight change in his voice. He'd spoken the words slowly, as if he was having difficulty comprehending.

"Siske. Did he come back? Did you have trouble with him? Damn, I should have picked you up. What happened?"

There was no way to avoid his anger, she knew. He wouldn't understand why she wasn't with him on such an important evening in his life. She'd let him down. He'd feel only the disappointment, nothing else. "I was getting ready to leave, to meet you. The other store owners came. They wanted a meeting, Pete. I thought I'd be done and would get to the restaurant on time. They're all still terribly frightened, but they finally came to talk."

He was silent.

"They've been so reluctant. I knew that if we didn't have the meeting at that moment, they might change their minds."

"You couldn't tell them that you had to be somewhere else?" he asked, disliking the annoyed tone in his own voice, yet unable to battle it. "You couldn't have arranged to meet them later tonight?"

Of course, she thought, he'd taken the logical path. How could she make him understand the fear that all those people had fought before they'd come into her store? "I doubt they'd have mustered up their courage twice. This was too important—"

"*This* was important to me, too."

"I know it is." Irritated, she fought to remain calm, sensing that if she lost her temper, then his would flare. "But there wasn't any way for me to—"

"You had a choice."

"I really didn't. Don't you understand?"

"I understand that you said you love me, but when I need you, you aren't here. I understand that you don't think about the consequences of anything. You didn't worry about how embarrassing this is for me."

"That's not true. I didn't do this deliberately," she shot back.

He released a harsh sigh. "I'm sure you didn't. You haven't changed, have you?"

"I never said that I had, Pete." She swallowed hard, feeling the tightness in her throat constricting.

"Moment-to-moment. That's how you lead your life."

She ignored his sarcasm. "Is Mr. Bryant upset?"

"Do you care?"

"It doesn't matter about me. You care."

"Too much," he said, not thinking about Bryant, not really caring about him or the woman with him. "I was worried, wondering what happened to you."

"What did you say to them?"

"I made apologies and excuses to Bryant."

"My being late didn't sit well with him?"

"He might overlook your being late. But there's a journalist here who's snapping at anything that resembles a way to grab the brass ring. She wants more for her story than the dry facts about the firm's southwestern office. She wants something that will make the readers wonder if Bryant and Bryant's employees are as untarnished as Bryant claims."

"And I provided her with grist for the mill," Ariel finished for him. He didn't answer. His irritation with the reporter made sense to her. He had casually mentioned that the woman wanted to spice her story with contradictory facts about the company's honorable and scrupulous reputation. Still, Ariel frowned, confused. "Why would she concern herself with me? How could I be associated with the firm?"

Pete tightened his jaw. "I announced that we were going to get married."

Now she understood. "Pete, I'd planned to be there on time." She sensed the futility in trying to explain. His silence coiled the knot in her stomach tighter. "It's late, but if I left right away, I could get there in a few minutes.''

Briefly he considered that he was overreacting, but logic fled from him at the moment. He hurt, and he wanted to avoid the emotion. "Never mind.''

"You don't want me to come?''

"You're right, Ariel. It is too late.''

The phone clicked in her ear. She gripped the receiver tighter. They'd failed the test. Hadn't she sensed that they would? Hadn't she known that if the time came when he relied on her to do the right thing, she'd fail? She hadn't slipped into the slots while married to Jonathan, either. She'd tried, but they'd been uncomfortable. "Moment-to-moment," Pete had said. Yes, she did live her life that way. She saw what existed in front of her at the moment, and he viewed life with long-range vision. For a little while she'd tried to believe they'd make it. She'd looked through his eyes, seen the happiness she had with him, and had believed it could be theirs forever. She'd clung to all the wonderful moments, wanting to believe that this time was different. But nothing had changed. Neither of them was right or wrong, just too different for them to ever make each other happy.

She set down the receiver and turned to join the others. The ache spiraled through her, hurting as much as it had the first time.

Pete returned to the table as the waiter was serving the chateaubriand. His throat was dry, and he wondered if he could force down the food.

"Was that Ms. Hammond?" Bryant asked.

Pete's orderly life felt jumbled, his pride raw from the bruises. Had he pushed too hard? Had arrogance gotten the best of him? He'd wanted everything—everything his way.

"Peter?"

He refocused on Bryant. "Yes, it was. She was detained," he said in a calm and controlled voice because he'd programmed himself to react that way to anger and frustration, but his stomach still churned.

"I'm sorry to hear that."

Bryant's voice was like a distant echo, his words running together as if he were speaking in a foreign tongue. He continued to talk and smile, his gaze swinging from Pete to Carol Jamison. Then he stopped, a look of expectation on his face as he stared at Pete.

"You must be pleased," Carol Jamison said, her expression similar to a defeated soldier's.

Pete nodded. What should he be pleased about? His world had turned topsy-turvy again.

"When you mentioned that you were asking a young woman to join us," Bryant went on, "I'd hoped that she'd be someone who would share in the joy of your good news. Since she's to be your wife, if Ms. Hammond had been able to come, she obviously would have."

"Sir?"

"Being your fiancée, she would have a vested interest in your future and would share in our little celebration," he said, nodding to the waiter.

Pete stared at the bottle of champagne. What were they celebrating? What was there to be happy about?

Bryant waited while the waiter poured a round, then raised the thin-stemmed glass.

Pete did what was expected. He'd always done what people expected. He was his father's son, not his mother's. She whirled through life, not caring what people thought, not caring who she hurt.

"To Bryant and Bryant's newest senior consultant," J.C. announced as a toast.

Pete watched glasses click against each other. So he'd succeeded; he'd gotten what he'd wanted most in his life.

But had he? he wondered, feeling no joy.

The evening dragged. He made polite conversation, managed timely smiles, but he felt no happiness. After he took Bryant and the journalist back to their hotels, he began driving. He drove with no destination in mind. Rain spotted the front window of his car. There was no sunshine this time as there should have been. All those years of hard work had paid off. The day had been an important one in his life, and he sat alone, watching raindrops plop against the window. He didn't know where to go or whom to see. Who cared but him that he was the youngest senior consultant with B and B?

He'd receive publicity, even favorable publicity from Carol Jamison. He'd be swamped with new clients who would view such success for a man of thirty-one as a barometer of his wisdom and intelligence and knowledge. If he could succeed like that for himself, what could he do for them?

Pete opened the car door and stood in the rain, letting it pelt against him. He needed the splash in the face to counter the numbness within. His brain told him to celebrate, but a heavy, depressing emptiness warred with the idea. He had everything he wanted. And he had nothing—he didn't have her.

Like a wound-up mechanical doll, he crossed the street, not thinking about where he was going.

He stood at the bottom of wooden stairs and stared at a familiar crack in the bottom one. At fifteen, he'd dropped a seventy-pound dumbbell on that step. The freshly painted wood had cracked. He'd expected his father's anger. Instead, with his usual wisdom, Evan had stared long and hard at the step and simply said that some things weren't strong enough to withstand certain pressure. The step had been painted many times since then, but the crack remained forever.

Slowly, Pete climbed the stairs and then rang the bell. Was it too late? Was his father in bed? Was he alone? Pete smiled wryly, realizing that he could be disturbing his father and Virginia during an intimate moment.

The door eased open slowly.

Evan peeked out at him. "Pete?" Quickly he unlatched the chain and flung open the door. "It's one in the morning."

"Can I come in?" he asked while he looked down his father's lean form. When had he bought a red silk robe with his initial embroidered on it?

"Of course." Evan grabbed his arm, urging him into the living room. "Coffee or a drink?"

"I'd like the drink," he answered, following Evan toward the kitchen. "But I'll take coffee. When did you get that robe?"

Evan grinned. "A far cry from my old flannel one, isn't it? Ginnie bought it for me."

Pete smiled for his father.

Reaching for a cup from the cupboard, Evan glanced back at him. "I've been told that red is a statement of..."

"Passion."

Evan made an embarrassed face. "So I've been told. Sit down."

Pete kept his voice low. "Is Virginia here?"

"No, not this evening. Why?"

"I didn't want to interrupt."

Evan pulled out a chair across from him. "Didn't you have that dinner meeting with Bryant tonight?"

Pete nodded. "I got the promotion."

"That's wonderful," Evan started, smiling wide with pride. The smile faded quickly. "You aren't pleased?"

"I feel like hell."

"It's what you wanted, isn't it?"

"Do we ever know what we really want?"

Evan squinted slightly. "It's too early in the morning for me to do such deep pondering. Why don't you tell me plain and simple what is wrong?"

"I wanted Ariel." The admission was spoken on a ragged sigh. "I wanted her in my life, and that isn't going to happen."

"What did you do?"

He raised his eyes. "Nothing. I didn't do anything. She did. She was supposed to be at the restaurant. She didn't show. She was too busy," he said, releasing the anger he'd stifled for hours.

"You're still losing me."

"She promised to be there and she didn't come."

"Why didn't she?"

"Some meeting of the store owners."

"An important meeting?"

"She thought so. She thought it was important enough to let me down. She didn't care enough about me or my feelings to worry about what I'd feel when she didn't show up. All that had mattered to her was what she was doing at that moment."

"Didn't she call?"

"Yeah, she called." Pete knew he wasn't being fair to Ariel or honest with his father, but telling him about Siske would complicate his explanation. He'd have to relate recent incidences calmly. He didn't feel calm. Pride demanded indignation. "Late. She called late. She didn't give a damn about the consequences of what she was doing to me."

"Trust is awfully important in a relationship. Sometimes, even when something seems wrong to you, you have to trust that what the other person is doing is probably right."

"You really believe that?"

"If you love each other." Evan pushed the sugar bowl toward him. "Do you want something to eat?"

Pete shook his head.

"I'm older than you, so I suppose that means I'm a little slower. I never thought of myself as slow, but I'm having a difficult time following you, understanding your anger. You got the promotion, didn't you?"

"I told you I did."

"So she didn't do anything to hurt your career?"

"To hell with the career. We're not talking about that." Pete pushed back the chair and wheeled around toward the kitchen window. The night was dark. Streams of moisture flowed down the windowpane. "It doesn't matter that everything worked out all right. It might not have, because she can't look beyond the moment."

"You're hurt by what could have happened?"

Pete heard his father's disbelief. Of all people, why didn't he understand?

"I would say that she's the kind of woman who gives a great deal of herself to other people," Evan went on.

"Yes, she does. But she's ruled by her emotions. She doesn't think. I mean, she doesn't consider tomorrow. To her all that matters is today." Pete whirled around and faced him. "She's like—"

"Who? Your mother?" At Pete's nod, his father's frown deepened. "You don't really believe that."

"Yes, I do."

"Because of one missed dinner?" Evan asked, looking amazed.

Pete's voice was laced with harsh pain. "Yes, because of one missed dinner. One of many if we married."

Evan sighed. "Aren't you judging her in advance?"

"Don't we have a guideline to go by?" Pete flared back. "I remember what it was like. Did you think because I was only seven that I didn't ache inside when she left us? I cried, too, Dad. But she didn't give a damn about us. She left us for some man, one of many who never made her happy. She couldn't have left if she had thought about anything but what she'd felt then, on that day, at that moment."

"Pete, she left me, not you."

"No, she left both of us," he said firmly. Sadness flashed in his father's eyes, assuring Pete that he was right. "I'm glad you're happy with Virginia. And I hope she never disappoints you like Ariel has me."

"Disappoint? Is that what Ariel has done to you?"

Evan's clipped, critical tone cut deep into Pete's thoughts. "Yes. Hasn't she proved that she only thinks about right now? She isn't concerned with tomorrow."

"I wonder," Evan said softly. He reached forward for his coffee cup. "You talk about disappointment. I wonder," he repeated, "if she was disappointed years ago."

Pete met his gaze with a quizzical one.

"I wonder if she planned tomorrows with you—before you walked away from her. You're awfully quick to do that again. I wonder why."

Evan's last statement had lingered in Pete's mind as he drove home. He was exhausted, mentally and physically, but instead of going to bed, he sat in a chair in the living room. He listened to the rain. It stirred old and new memories, good memories.

At what point had he crossed all of them out? Had he been waiting for this moment with her? Had he expected her to do something that emphasized all the differences between them? Had he been fair with her? Or honest with himself?

Because of his mother, he'd looked with disfavor on Virginia's relationship with his father. He saw similarities in Virginia and his mother, but they weren't bad traits. They were all the good traits that he'd remembered and mourned when his mother had left.

And he'd seen similar traits in Ariel. He'd been drawn to her six years before because of her quick laughter, her bright outlook, her adventurous streak. Because of her, he'd sky-dived and had hiked up a mountain to a lake that only the more spirited campers ever saw.

He'd walked away from her once. He'd made the exit quick and firm by moving to New York. He hadn't asked her what she wanted. He'd decided that she wanted something he couldn't offer, so he'd left her. Then he'd longed for her. For months he'd hurt badly for her. The pain had never really gone away. Wasn't that why he'd really returned to Albuquerque? And yet he was ready to rush away again.

Pete leaned back in the chair and closed his eyes. She wasn't the one who'd wanted nothing more than a moment-to-moment relationship. He was. On a long breath, he let the pain of honesty surge through him. He was afraid. He'd been afraid from the beginning, afraid she'd leave him. So he'd left first.

Chapter Thirteen

Ariel had arrived home in a temper, angry at Peter and herself. She slammed things around—a dresser drawer, a book on a table, any door handy. Then she wept.

She knew she wouldn't always make the right decision, at least, not for Pete's way of thinking. But then she hadn't really had a chance this time. She'd seen that entourage of five, six with her mother included, and she'd sensed that they'd battled some of the same dragons that she had. They'd fought insurmountable fear, the urge to run and pretend everything would work out even if they didn't get involved. They'd faced truth, knowing they didn't have a choice. And neither had she. She'd known the courage that all of them had stretched within themselves to find. And at that moment when they'd filed into her store, she'd forgotten everything else but their brave action to stand together.

Even with the outcome of her actions known now, she knew that she'd do the same again. What options had she had? she asked herself. The night was a restless one as she repeatedly wrestled with that question.

At midmorning of the next day, she dragged herself from the bed. She'd considered burying her head under the pillow until the memory of last night and the suffocating heartache subsided. The idea seemed childish. No huddling beneath blankets could resurrect any emotion but the empty one that was making her feel as if she were in limbo.

Tears no longer brimmed her eyes; she doubted that she had any left. She'd grieved for a loss as intense as the death of a loved one.

And now there was nothing.

After showering and dressing, she drove to the police station. A fatiguing emptiness accompanied her. As she sat in Detective Hernandez's office, she fought against apathy and concentrated on his plan to catch Siske.

"Be careful," Hernandez said for what seemed the tenth time. "I'll be near with some of my men. As soon as money is exchanged, we'll take over."

Ariel nodded, but her mind briefly skipped to thoughts of Pete. She swallowed the tightness in her throat, refusing to cry again. Hernandez would have misunderstood. He'd have thought that she wasn't strong enough for the task ahead of her. And how would she have explained herself? How could she have assured him that her tears weren't from fear for her own safety? Her tears were for two people who'd loved and lost.

"Janice will come to your store later today and pretend to buy something in case Siske is watching," the detective told her.

Ariel tucked a hand in her pocket to veil her nervousness and glanced at the dark-haired woman standing near the door. About the same age as Ariel, she had the bright smile of a kindergarten teacher.

"When she gets there, she'll plant several of these in various places in your store." He showed her a microphone the size of a hearing aid.

Ariel remained silent for a moment as what he was telling her finally sank in. "I don't have to wear one?" she asked, surprised.

"We'd prefer that you didn't."

Relief calmed her somewhat. "I thought I'd have to."

"We don't want to put you in any danger if we can avoid it. And sometimes during tense moments, people perspire more than usual. The perspiration interferes with transmission."

Ariel nodded, not really concerned with the technical problems.

Hernandez indicated a tall, handsome, gray-haired man who stood beside Janice. "Frank, two other officers, and I will be in the surveillance van parked near your store." He settled on the edge of his desk, bringing his eyes level with hers. "We don't want you to take any unnecessary chances tonight. Talk to Siske, lead him with questions, but don't get him jumpy. He's resorted to violence on a few occasions. We don't want to see that directed at you."

Ariel balled the hand in her pocket. "I don't plan on playing the hero."

Hernandez grinned widely at her. "For not trying, I'd say you're doing a fine job of it."

Ariel smiled bleakly, then turned and left for home. At six that evening she would return to the store and open it before Siske arrived. But for now she lacked the energy for anything. She knew depression was controlling her, but she felt too drained to fight it.

Sunshine warmed her flesh, but the cold chill of an autumn day rippled through her as she walked toward home. Strangling tension and apprehension accompanied her. She might regret what she was going to do that evening, but she'd never be sorry about the time shared with Pete. Despite the heartache now, she'd cling to the memory of the magic they'd shared. She'd remember only the good times, and she'd always wonder why that enchantment had disappeared with a swiftness that had left her speechless. Life wasn't a fairy tale, yet some wizard seemed to have cursed them, letting them sample happiness at its fullest for short periods of time before returning to wreak his stunning vengeance. In one evening, all the joy she'd known had been stolen from her, and she really didn't understand why.

Standing on the bottom step outside her apartment door, Pete followed her approach as she started down the steps. Her head bent, she dug into her purse for her keys. As she looked up and met his gaze, a flickering of emotion flashed across her face. Hurt. He stared at her eyes, saw the pain, and knew he'd caused it. Whatever logical plan he'd had slipped away as guilt gripped him.

Ariel froze. For a second she was paralyzed. Her first thought was how tired he looked, and how sad.

She tried hard not to jump to conclusions. Her moods had swung from heartbroken to sad and back again ever since her phone conversation with him. Right now too many emotions plagued her. Mostly she yearned for him to open his arms to her.

Instead neither of them moved.

Seconds ticked by. In the distance she heard the wail of a siren, the shout of a child's voice, the gunning of a car engine. Sunlight beat at her back. The fragrance of daisies drifted over her. Yet her world narrowed to the small space that separated them.

"Could I come in?" Pete asked softly, hooking his fingers into the change pocket of his jeans to resist reaching out to her. He knew she deserved more than his touch.

She gave a quick nod and smiled, but he noted the warmth didn't sweep across her face. His heart quickened to a light, fluttery beat. Following her in, he was nagged by one thought. What if she refused him now? Now that he'd finally recognized the core of their problem.

Ariel moved into the room quickly, fearful that if he remained close to the door, he wouldn't take more than a step into the room.

"I went to the store and..." he began, but his voice weakened as she stood near a chair and faced him, shoving her bangs away from her forehead in a familiar nervous habit. "I always seem to hurt you."

"Funny," she said weakly, "I was going to say I do the same to you." She saw that pain darkened his eyes. "Unwittingly, I disrupt the smooth order of your life. What happened with Bryant? Did he—did you get offered the senior position?"

Pete nodded.

Her face brightened. "I'm glad." She wanted to hug him. She wanted to lead him into another room and celebrate, but she couldn't take one step closer to him. "I worried." She took a step back and sought a chair, because her legs felt wobbly. "You've worked so hard."

Despite everything, Pete marveled, she cared enough to ask, but then he'd never doubted her depth of giving and caring. "Yeah, I did a lot of worrying, too. About me. About presenting a sterling image." He extended an open hand. "I should have been thinking about you. What you were doing." He turned away. "But then, you know how to love better than I do. You understand that love really means caring about others more than yourself."

Taking a deep breath, Ariel curled her hands over the armrests.

"I've never really understood love," he said softly, staring out the window. "I told you that I loved you, but when I had to face what it really was, I ran from it. But then, I had run from it before. I'm the one who's afraid to make a commitment, a real one." He released a soft, mirthless laugh. "The irony is amazing. I left before to avoid being hurt, and I hurt myself. And you," he said, turning to face her. "I've been so damn self-righteous that I couldn't see the truth even when I stared right at it."

She closed the distance until only inches separated them. "Pete," she said softly, touching his cheek.

"No." He shook his head. "I need to say it all. I've been afraid of feeling the same hurt that I remembered when my mother left. Because of that, I've skirted every chance with you to have the love that I claimed I wanted." He leaned forward and pressed his forehead to hers. "I've been so afraid of losing you that I grabbed the first opportunity I could to leave first. And I'm sorry. I never meant to hurt you."

She made a small sound as he slipped his arms around her.

"I can't do without you again," he whispered brokenly. "I don't want to."

"Hold me. Love me," she whispered.

"I do." He buried his face in her hair. "And I'll never let you forget that," he added softly, drawing her down to the rug with him. He started to say more, but her mouth was on his. All doubts and fears subsided as she gave him her love, just as she always had. Before now he'd been afraid to receive the intensity of her giving. Unknowingly he'd always held a part of himself from her, protectively shielding himself by not totally trusting her. She had him completely now. His heart was hers.

Swift and demanding, love mingled with need, surpassing simple desire. He was lost, tumbling into a magical wonderland with her. His mind filled with her scent, her taste, her touch. Hands that meant to be gentle bruised with urgency. He kissed her full and hard. Then his mouth moved everywhere, his voice ragged as he cursed their clothing.

Strong, hard thighs pressed against soft, firm ones. Sighs mingled. Caresses changed and became demands.

Her desperation matched his; her need to touch became as insistent as his own. And the headiness of pleasure given and returned and shared enveloped them.

She wanted to tempt, to torment, to please. She brushed her fingers over the dampness and the smoothness of his flesh. She knew now that there would be no more tests. They couldn't fail. They had a love strong enough to withstand any argument or disappointment or failure. They had a love that included sharing. No matter what came their way, neither of them would ever be alone. They had each other now.

Mouths explored, hers following a similiar, curious trail, a familiar one she'd wandered before. Caresses became possessive as she journeyed with him to a place where reason and reality slipped away. A loving madness took control.

She lost track of time and place. Sunlight streamed in from the window, but its warmth felt secondary to the blaze sweeping through her.

Naked on the rug, they strained against each other.

Arching, her body melted against his, and she gasped, struggling for the simple normalcy of breathing when he entered her.

She followed the commands of his urging hands. Beneath him, she taunted and invited. With him she raced breathlessly to a finish, yet she longed to savor the joys along the way. As one with him, she pressed closer to reach the end. Then waves of sensation lapped over them, a final assurance that they belonged together, one in mind and body and soul.

For a long time they clung to each other. Sunshine no longer filled the room. As darkness began to close around them, she stirred against him, burying her face in his neck, not wanting to leave his side.

Feeling her movement, he reached out and closed his fingers over her wrist. "Stay."

She knelt beside him and stared into his eyes. Seeing the puzzlement flickering in their darkness, she kissed him quickly and forced a smile to banish the look from his face before she pulled away.

As she headed toward the bathroom, Pete cradled his arm beneath his head and watched her movements until she disappeared from sight. Her heat lingered on his body. He let the past moments seep into his mind, a keepsake of their beginning. A real beginning this time, now that all fears and doubts were finally exorcised. Beneath him, the carpet felt scratchy. He smiled, realizing he hadn't noticed it before. For several moments he stayed perfectly still, too content to move.

From the bathroom, he heard running water, then humming.

His gaze shifted to the bedroom. Suddenly he laughed softly as he saw where she'd placed the stuffed animal he'd given her. Somehow she'd propped the dragon in the arm of the sentry knight standing near her bed. The sight was humorous, the grinning dragon looking docile and pleased to be held by the knight.

Pete's smile slipped as a more serious thought took shape. Some dragons were real, and he needed to be near her when they appeared. He wouldn't let her down. He'd be near for her just as he knew she'd be at his side when he had dragons to slay.

She was still humming when she emerged from the bedroom. Pete tilted his head back to look at her. "Even upside down you look beautiful. Even overdressed," he added, noting her jeans and blouse.

She couldn't resist moving to him and kissing him. Though a light kiss, it was intimate. She drew away with some regret, knowing that she could slip back down beside him too easily.

"I have to leave," she said, sitting back on her heels.

Pete stared hard at her. Her smile didn't reach her eyes. More important, he remembered that she'd been humming. He bolted to a sitting position. "Where are you going?"

"I have a meeting with Siske," she answered quietly.

"Tonight!" he declared with alarm.

She wished she had words to calm him, but she was far from calm herself. "In a little while."

Pete grabbed for his shirt.

Ariel tilted back her head. Puzzled, she stared up at him. "What are you doing?"

"I'm going with you."

Ariel pushed to a stand. "You can't."

"I am." He tugged on his jeans. "I'm not letting you do this alone."

"You can't go with me." Her tone made the statement unequivocal.

"Watch me."

"I won't be gone..." She frowned as he uncharacteristically wiggled his feet, minus socks, into his sneakers.

"I'm not going to listen. Not for one more minute," he said, looking down and snapping his jeans.

"I'm not frightened," she lied, not wanting him to get involved.

He released an astonished, mirthless laugh. "Well, I'm scared to death for you. He's playing hard ball. Don't you understand that he's not fooling around?"

"You can't afford to get involved in something like this."

"Wrong." His eyes met hers as he gripped her upper arms. "During all the years we weren't together, I never stopped loving you. From now on, we share. The good and the bad times. I'm not taking any chances now. I'm going with you," he said firmly.

"Hernandez isn't going to like this."

"I'll handle him."

"I'm sure you will." Amusement edged her voice.

As she stepped toward the door he curled his hand on the back of her neck, halting her.

Ariel looked up at him. "Do you know what is going to happen to your life?"

Lightly his lips touched hers. "I'm going to get everything I ever wanted."

Detective Hernandez scowled at Pete's refusal to budge from Ariel's store. Pete promised not to get in the way of the police department's plan, but he was staying. He'd hide in the storeroom to be close to Ariel while she talked to Siske.

Pete stood firm, realizing the detective had only two choices—arrest him for obstructing justice or acquiesce to his request. After Pete promised not to sprout a red cape, Hernandez reluctantly agreed to let him stay.

The waiting, Ariel reflected, was the hardest part. At 9:25 she stood behind the counter in her store, jumping at the slightest noise.

"Any sight of him?" Pete whispered from his position behind a large crate filled with oxidized copper statues.

"No," Ariel answered, trying not to move her lips too much. "Stop asking me questions. If he's—He's here." She spoke low, moving to the designated section of the cash register counter where a microphone was jammed between the leaves of an overflowing philodendron. Briefly she scanned her store, trying to remember where the several other microphones were located. If Siske moved away from the counter, she had to maneuver him near another microphone.

She stood motionless, watching Siske enter the room. A cloud of smoke from his cigar drifted into the store ahead of him. Ariel sniffed disdainfully.

"Do you have it?" Siske asked.

"Yes."

"Wise of you," he said, closing the distance between them to stand on the other side of the counter. "I wouldn't want anything to happen to such a pretty woman."

"I'm sure nothing bothers you. Whether it's slashing one of Mr. Calhoun's paintings or breaking my window."

Pete cringed, wishing she didn't sound so indignant, but he guessed she'd been briefed on what to say and how to react.

Siske snorted a laugh. "Mr. Calhoun required a stronger sales pitch than the others." He puffed hard on the cigar, eyeing her, making Ariel want to squirm. "So you've all talked?"

Ariel stood firm. "Did you think that we wouldn't?"

"No, I expected you would share news of your unfortunate accidents."

"That's what this money is for, isn't it?" she said, reaching into her purse for the envelope stuffed with government money. "This will prevent more of those so-called unfortunate accidents, Mr. Siske."

"How formal," Siske said in a laughing tone. "There's no need for that. Just be prompt with the money."

"Or what?" Ariel goaded him. "Will you tie a cement bag to my feet and dump me in the river?"

Siske chuckled. "You watch too many gangster movies. In time, you'll learn to do this with less reluctance."

"I doubt it. I don't like being threatened. I especially don't like having to pay you money."

"But you will."

Ariel presented her best defeated tone. "What choice do I have? Any of us. The Trembles or Mr. Calhoun or Mr. Varquez. We can't fight someone like you."

In his raspy voice, amusement came out on a chilling tone. "You exaggerate."

"Yes, I suppose you could have done much worse than hit Mr. Calhoun on the head."

"Unlike you, he needed more convincing to accept my services."

"You get paid to protect us from you."

He laughed. "I'm going to make you my last pickup. I'm finding your comments amusing."

"Here," she said, "take the money and leave me alone."

Paper rustled as the envelope exchanged hands.

"Until next month. Same time."

She felt the dampness of perspiration in the small of her back, but she reined in her fear. "And if I refuse to make another payment?"

"You don't look stupid. Are you telling me I haven't made myself clear to you?"

Ariel raised her chin defiantly. Pete had told her that the look gave the impression that she was offering someone her chin as a target. Ariel hardly wanted Siske to slug her, but if a tilt of her chin could annoy someone as controlled and easygoing as Pete usually was, it should fuel anger in Siske.

"You push, then I'll push back," he snapped threateningly.

"I'm not frightened."

He released a mirthless laugh and fondled the envelope. "I can tell that," he gibed. "But..." He leaned across the counter, bringing his face within inches of Ariel's. She wrinkled her nose at the sight of his stained teeth as he added, "You give me trouble and I'll break more than a stained-glass window."

Ariel opened her mouth to snarl a retort at him. Instead she cringed as he suddenly spun around, responding to the click of the door.

As it flung open he whirled back, rolled over the top of the counter, then hit the highly polished floor and ran for the back exit.

Police shouts to halt went unheeded. Panic swept through Ariel as Pete shot out from his hiding place and dived, flying at Siske's back. They fell to the floor with a loud thump.

Commanding shouts echoed throughout the store along with the scurrying footsteps of uniformed men rushing toward the storeroom. Glass shattered as stemware was knocked over, and the bell above the door tinkled continually as more police rushed toward Pete and Siske.

Tangled, they rolled and banged against a support crate. She heard a crash when two stacked crates tipped and then fell to the storeroom floor. Then she could no longer see Pete.

Panicky, she scrambled to rush around the counter. Hernandez's meaty arm blocked her. Endless seconds followed as she stretched to see past the uniformed backs. When she spotted the top of Pete's dark head, a dizzying relief swept through her. A rush of movement gave her a clearer view. He looked disheveled but uninjured from his tumble.

Leaning back against the counter, she closed her eyes. She felt weak. The sensation surprised her. She'd never fainted in her life. She didn't plan to now, either, she reminded herself, but she was grateful for the strong arms suddenly enclosing her in a warm, protective cocoon.

Swaying against Pete, she gave in to all the tension of the past few minutes. Tears streamed down her cheeks as she looked up at him. "Why did you do that?" she asked, wanting to scold and cling to him at the same time. "You could have been hurt."

He tightened his hold on her and laughed softly. "Impulse." Catching a tear on her cheek with his fingertip, he repeated, "Pure impulse." He crushed her to him, relief over her safety making him tremble. "I love you."

"I love you, too," said a muffled male voice from the depths of the philodendron.

Frowning, Pete reared back and turned a startled glance at the plant, then at Detective Hernandez.

Hernandez raised one thick, dark eyebrow. "I hope you mean what you say to her."

A crooked grin flashed across Pete's face. "I'm on tape?"

Hernandez's deep voice lowered. "Anything you say to her will be between you, her, and the fellows in our surveillance van."

Pete slipped an arm around her waist. "Ariel, let's get out of here."

Just as eager to escape the chaos surrounding them, she nodded and then blinked, responding to a flash of light from the doorway. Ariel turned a worried look in the direction of a uniformed officer blocking a photographer's entrance to her store.

A camera in his hand, a man rubbernecked from the doorway. "I heard the call on my scanner. Come on, let me in to get the story." As the officer stood firm, the man pestered him, "Then at least give me the name of the hero."

Ariel frowned up at Pete. "I think you're going to be in print again," she said worriedly. "J.C.—"

Pete urged her toward the back exit. "Forget about him, right now."

"Pete, J.C. might not—"

He smiled down at her and tugged her closer as they ambled through the storeroom.

Briefly, Ariel glanced at Siske, who was handcuffed and flanked by two policemen.

Pete touched her chin and insisted she look at him instead. "I like you. Have I told you that?"

She tilted her head questioningly. "No more doubts?"

"None," he assured her. "No one takes a risk like you did with Siske and doesn't care about what happens tomorrow. I like you a lot," he repeated, kissing the bridge of her nose.

"You're acting strange."

Outside, he drew her into his arms. "I just wanted you to know that."

Ariel slid her arms beneath his and around his back. "You've told me that you love me."

"I can do better than tell you." He smiled down at her and urged her toward the car. "Let's go home, and I'll show you how much."

Epilogue

Pancakes?" Ariel stretched on the bed beside Pete, tangling her leg with his.

"Too messy," he drawled sleepily, but as strands of her hair tickled his bare shoulder, he wondered if he had enough flour for batter.

She laughed huskily, a sexy, lazy laugh that made him smile.

He hadn't opened his eyes yet, but he was smiling. Shifting, he lowered his lips to the faint spray of freckles on her nose. "When?"

"When what?" she murmured.

"Do you want to get married?"

"When do you?"

"Today."

She opened her eyes. His were intense. "Is that possible?"

"Anything is possible."

Her lips curved with a slow, enticing smile. Slowly he lowered his mouth to hers, but the shrill of the phone jarred both of them from their languid mood.

Ariel sighed and slid down, yanking the sheet over her head.

On an annoyed oath, Pete rolled away from her and glared at the ringing phone. "It's not even seven in the morning," he mumbled. "You'd think people would have more sense."

"Grumble, grumble," she said to herself, then smiled again. Contentment settled over her as she decided she could stand a touch of morning surliness when the rest of the day would bring such joy. Blissful, she buried her face in the pillow, but the extended silences in Pete's conversation piqued her curiosity. Ariel peeked out from under the sheet and stared at him.

He stroked her hair and mouthed exaggeratedly, "J.C."

Ariel pushed herself up beside him. His expression told her nothing. Anxiously she cocked her head close to his to hear Bryant.

"Ah, no, I hadn't heard." Pete spread his arm behind her to drape it around her shoulder and tuck her against him. "I'll look forward to seeing you again, too."

Worriedly, Ariel studied his face. Why would J.C. call so early? She waited only until Pete set down the receiver. "Why did he call?"

"Jamison. Remember her?" At Ariel's nod, he went on. "She felt it was her duty to inform him again about current events here and get his comment."

"She told him what happened last night?"

"We're in the newspaper, I guess. According to Bryant, our photograph and a story are on page one of the local news section."

She stared into his eyes. They were very black. "Pete, was he upset?"

He shifted his head on the pillow so he could see her clearly. "You'd have thought I was some kind of national hero. J.C. decided such heroic action would impress clients."

Ariel pulled back, propping an elbow on a pillow to rest her cheek against her knuckles. "What else? Tell me all."

"All is that he's pleased." He teasingly ran a finger from the base of her throat down to the top of the sheet and the shadow of flesh between her breasts. "Having one of his associates scuffle with a criminal to help the law verifies B and B's impeccable reputation. And then there's you." He bent forward, letting his mouth trace the same path. "He thinks you're wonderful," he murmured.

"That's what he said?" she asked lightly.

"Uh-huh. I told him that you were one in a million."

Ariel closed her eyes again. "He'd be impressed with that?" she asked lazily.

"Anything over six figures." Gently he kissed her once, then again.

She trembled, love and joy mingling together. He'd barely touched her, and she felt warm and excited. "I'd planned to get out of bed."

"Did you? Are you firm about that idea?" he asked, feeling her body warm beneath his touch.

"Actually, I'm a very flexible person."

"I know. Don't ever change."

Her stomach muscles tensed as his fingertips floated across her skin. "I won't, but I have one request."

"Anything." He smiled in response to her giggle.

"Don't you ever change."

He released a quick, astonished laugh. "After everything that's happened, you can say that?"

"Without hesitation."

"How did I live without you all those years?"

"That was yesterday." She kissed the curve of his shoulder. "All that matters now are tomorrows."

* * * * *

Silhouette Intimate Moments

WHEN OPPOSITES ATTRACT

Roberta Malcolm had spent her life on the Mescalero ranch. Then Hollywood—and Jed Pulaski—came to Mescalero, and suddenly everything changed.

Jed Pulaski had never met anyone like Rob Malcolm. Her forthright manner hid a woman who was beautiful, vibrant—and completely fascinating. But Jed knew their lives were as far apart as night from day, and only an all-consuming love could bring them together, forever, in the glory of dawn.

Look for Jed and Roberta's story in *That Malcolm Girl*, IM #253, Book Two of Parris Afton Bonds's Mescalero Trilogy, available this month only from Silhouette Intimate Moments. Then watch for Book Three, *That Mescalero Man* (December 1988), to complete the trilogy.

Silhouette Romance

LONG, TALL TEXANS

A Trilogy by Diana Palmer

Bestselling Diana Palmer has rustled up three rugged heroes in a trilogy sure to lasso your heart! The titles of the books are your introduction to these unforgettable men:

CALHOUN

In June, you met Calhoun Ballenger. He wanted to protect Abby Clark from the world, but could he protect her from himself?

JUSTIN

Calhoun's brother, Justin—the strong, silent type—had a second chance with the woman of his dreams, Shelby Jacobs, in August.

TYLER

October's long, tall Texan is Shelby's virile brother, Tyler, who teaches shy Nell Regan to trust her instincts—especially when they lead her into his arms!

Don't miss TYLER, the last of three gripping stories from Silhouette Romance!

Silhouette Desire ®

CHILDREN OF DESTINY

A trilogy by Ann Major

Three power-packed tales of irresistible passion and undeniable fate created by Ann Major to wrap your heart in a legacy of love.

PASSION'S CHILD — September

Years ago, Nick Browning nearly destroyed Amy's life, but now that the child of his passion —the child of her heart—was in danger, Nick was the only one she could trust....

DESTINY'S CHILD — October

Cattle baron Jeb Jackson thought he owned everything and everyone on his ranch, but fiery Megan MacKay's destiny was to prove him wrong!

NIGHT CHILD — November

When little Julia Jackson was kidnapped, young Kirk MacKay blamed himself. Twenty years later, he found her . . . and discovered that love could shine through even the darkest of nights.

Don't miss PASSION'S CHILD, DESTINY'S CHILD and NIGHT CHILD, three thrilling Silhouette Desires designed to heat up chilly autumn nights!

SD-445

Silhouette Special Edition

COMING NEXT MONTH

#481 CHAMPAGNE FOR BREAKFAST—Tracy Sinclair
Raoul Ruiz, Mexico City's most eligible bachelor, generously salvaged
Lacey Scott's vacation. Then he passionately romanced her, proving as
intoxicating—and elusive—as the bubbles in a glass of champagne.

#482 THE PLAYBOY AND THE WIDOW—Debbie Macomber
More earthy than beautiful, more wholesome than sexy, housewife and
mother Diana Collins wasn't playboy Cliff Howard's type. So why did he
find the plucky widow irresistibly enticing?

#483 WENDY WYOMING—Myrna Temte
That heavenly voice! Who *was* Cheyenne, Wyoming's sexy new deejay?
Jason Wakefield pumped his pal, radio insider Melody Hunter—but
suddenly he wanted Mel more than the answer!

#484 EDGE OF FOREVER—Sherryl Woods
Dana Brantley had sacrificed intimacy for refuge from a traumatic,
haunting past. But insistent Nick Verone and his adorable ten-year-old son
kept pushing. Would the truth destroy their fragile union?

#485 THE BARGAIN—Patricia Coughlin
Vulnerable Lisa Bennett kept pursuers at bay, so wily Sam Ravenal played
hard to get. Intriguing her with pirate lore and hidden treasure, Sam freed
her anchored imagination . . . and baited her heart.

#486 BOTH SIDES NOW—Brooke Hastings
To buttoned-down Bradley Fraser, Sabrina Lang was reckless,
irresponsible . . . and dangerously alluring. Then, on a Himalayan
adventure, Brad spied her softer side—and fell wholeheartedly in love!

AVAILABLE NOW:

#475 SKIN DEEP
Nora Roberts

#476 TENDER IS THE KNIGHT
Jennifer West

#477 SUMMER LIGHT
Jude O'Neill

**#478 REMEMBER THE
DAFFODILS**
Jennifer Mikels

#479 IT MUST BE MAGIC
Maggi Charles

**#480 THE EVOLUTION OF
ADAM**
Pat Warren